WOOL

Cumbria
County Council

Libraries, books and more...........

Please return/renew this item by the last date shown.
Library items may also be renewed by phone on
030 33 33 1234 (24hours) or via our website

www.cumbria.gov.uk/libraries

Cumbria Libraries
CLIC
Interactive Catalogue

Ask for a CLIC password

BY MARK LOWERY

The Roman Garstang Disasters
The Jam Doughnut that Ruined My Life
The Chicken Nugget Ambush
Attack of the Woolly Jumper

and

Socks Are Not Enough
Pants Are Everything

MARK LOWERY

PRESS

First published in Great Britain in 2017 by
Piccadilly Press
80-81 Wimpole St, London W1G 9RE
www.piccadillypress.co.uk

A CIP catalogue record for this book is
available from the British Library.

ISBN: 978-1-84812-582-7
also available as an ebook
1 3 5 7 9 10 8 6 4 2

Typeset by Palimpsest Book Production Ltd, Falkirk, Stirlingshire
Printed and bound by Clays Ltd, St Ives Plc

Piccadilly Press is an imprint of Bonnier Zaffre Ltd,
a Bonnier Publishing company
www.bonnierpublishing.com

To Mrs Lowery and the Bambini

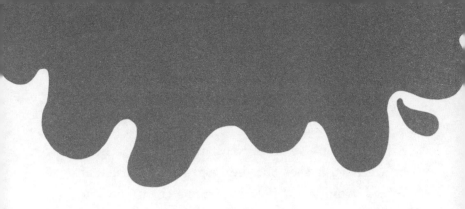

My name is Roman Garstang and I don't like clothes.

Now that's not the same as saying, 'I like **no clothes**.' I'm not weird. I definitely don't want to walk about in the nude, all pink and wobbly like a giant plucked chicken.

I just mean I'm not bothered about which clothes I wear and I've never understood people who are; especially when most fashion trends seem to be completely crackers.

Last month a pop star called Tara Krust went on stage wearing a dress made entirely out of slices of cheese. Yes, as in *actual* slices of *actual* cheese. I only know this because Rosie Taylor (AKA the Worst Person Who Ever Lived) brought a photo of her in to our class for show and tell, and made a speech about how 'brave' and 'clever' she was.

Brave and clever?

I don't think so. Tara Krust isn't exactly a hero or a genius, is she? She didn't protect a cluster of babies from a man-eating hamster, or invent something amazing and important like a reusable jam doughnut.

All she'd done was slap a few Dairylea slices onto herself like some kind of mad human cheeseburger. Personally I thought she looked like a total nutter. She only got away with it because she's a famous singer. Imagine if I went around wearing a waistcoat made out of mashed potato, or a pair of satsuma trousers, or a bobble hat made from lasagne. I'd get taken away in an ambulance.

It's official: fashion is pointless and stupid, and I don't get it.

But then again, clothes *can* have important jobs.

Firstly, they say a lot about you. For instance, Rosie Taylor sometimes wears a top with 'This Jumper Cost More Than Your House' printed on it in gold writing. Also a kid in my class called Kevin 'the Grand Old Puke of York' Harrison usually has a couple of dried-up sick stains on his togs if you look closely enough. And my sort-of best friend Darren Gamble (probably the naughtiest kid in Europe) likes T-shirts with the names of his favourite heavy metal bands on them. His current favourites are 'The Erupting Nappies', 'Razor Blade Ruth and the Tortured Piglets', and 'Death By Toilet'.

I'll let you decide what these clothes say about each of them.

Secondly, clothes can protect you. You can buy thick winter coats, bulletproof vests, anti-tortoise wellington boots, etc.

Yes, clothes can *save* your life – but I've recently discovered that they can also destroy it. And I should know. Last week I was exposed to the nastiest, cruellest, most violent object known to man.

A homemade woolly jumper.

A Strange and Deadly Weapon

When you think about it, woolly jumpers are all about making simple things extremely complicated. You take a few straightforward strands of wool, then you tie them into thousands of knots until you've got an awful item of clothing.

And that's exactly what the jumper did to me. It took my simple and straightforward life (go to school – eat doughnuts – go home – eat more doughnuts – repeat) and tangled it up into a mess.

OK, so I'll admit that maybe things weren't all that simple or straightforward before the jumper came along. A few weeks earlier, a single jam doughnut had made me shave a prize guinea pig and cover my girlfriend in wee, as well as causing a riot at an old people's tea party.

And then I'd been on a disastrous Year Six residential trip, where I was forced to eat nothing but disgusting chicken nuggets. Because of the nuggets:

I doubled my number of friends. This should've been a good thing, but 50% of my friends are still Darren Gamble.

I missed out on the zip wire because Kevin 'Grand Old Puke of York' Harrison threw up into my welly boot.

I was attacked by a trillion chickens.

Gamble made friends with a cow called Gusher and hid it in our tent.

On live TV, the cow covered Rosie Taylor
from head to toe in sloppy green poo. The
video clip 'Cow Toilet Girl' went viral on the
internet and had over eight million views in
seventy-two hours. She'd been desperate to
get her revenge on me ever since.

However, ten days later, my school routine had
returned to normal and jam doughnuts were back
on the menu. I was thrilled. But it was then, when
my guard was down, that the evil woolly jumper
struck.

MONDAY

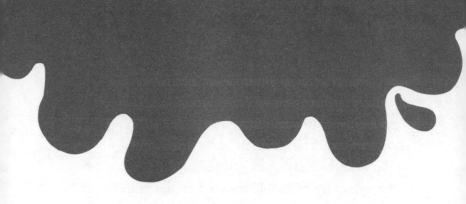

Morning

When I Learned about Royal Badgers and
Came Face to Face with Pure, Woolly Evil

It was a strange morning.

A couple of decent things had happened. Before
school, Mum and Dad had been busy so I'd had
to make my own packed lunch. I'd decided on a
delicious, balanced meal: two jam doughnuts (one
for each hand). And now, as we waited for our
teacher Mrs McDonald to come in and take the
register, I was sitting next to the good half of my
friends (i.e. Vanya Goyal, the coolest girl in the
whole class). These things should've made me
happy.

But I also had a few issues.

Firstly, I was tired. This was because Grandma had suddenly come to stay the day before. Now I love my grandma. But when she comes to stay she brings . . . **problems** with her.

I'd been kicked out of my bedroom and forced to sleep on a tiny inflatable mattress in the spare room. Unfortunately the mattress had a puncture so it went flat in no time. And, because it's ancient, it absolutely stank of meaty old sweat. Plus Grandma likes the heating in the house turned up to the temperature of the sun. It was about as comfortable as lying on top of a piece of bacon inside a frying pan.

As well as this, Grandma had brought me a present.

I don't want to sound ungrateful, but Grandma's presents are always rubbish. And this one was spectacularly dreadful. In fact, it was the worst present ever. Even worse than when Gamble gave me that dead pigeon for my birthday. But, because Grandma's a sweet old woman and I didn't want to hurt her feelings, I had to pretend I liked it. Later on, when she wasn't looking, I'd hidden it away before it could do any damage.

And what was this terrible gift?

Yep, you guessed it – a *woolly jumper*.

OK, it might not sound too bad, but you have no idea how dangerous this woolly jumper was. The problem was that neither did I, until it was far too late.

Animals

To kill time while the class waited for Mrs McDonald, the other half of my friends (Darren Gamble) was giving himself a tattoo on his forehead using a handwriting pen and the sharp point of a maths compass. Instead of stopping him, Miss Clegg, his one-to-one teaching assistant, was asleep with her head on the desk, snoring like a broken lawnmower.

Miss Clegg is meant to stop Gamble from being naughty but she doesn't try very hard at her job because she doesn't like Gamble much. One time I heard her say that she wished she lived in the olden days so that, when Gamble was bad, she could 'hit him with a stick or maybe chop off a few of his body parts'.

I'm not sure whether or not she was joking.

Everyone else in the class was chatting and laughing. Well, everyone apart from Rosie Taylor, that is. She was sitting alone on the table behind me. Whenever I turned my head, I could see her glaring angrily at me, her eyes glowing like two radioactive tomatoes.

She's always hated me but, since the Cow Pat Incident, she'd been worse than ever. She blamed me for it. I think this was a bit unfair. I mean, *I* didn't go to the toilet on her, did I?

This didn't seem to matter to Rosie, though. Ever since then, she'd spent all her free time trying to think of ways to get back at me. Last week she stuffed my PE trainers full of old tuna sandwiches and also spread a rumour that I have a 'curly-wurly winkle like a pig'.

I don't by the way.

Anyway, just as we were starting to hope that Mrs McDonald wasn't going to turn up at all, she burst into the room and cried, 'Stop what you're doing! I have an exciting announcement to make!'

Mrs McDonald was bright red and she looked ready to pop, just like a massive zit. Everyone immediately sat up straight. Even Miss Clegg woke up and wiped the drool off her chin.

'What is it, miss?' called out Gamble, who was bleeding slightly from the big letter D on his forehead. 'Has the new class pet been delivered?'

The excitement drained from Mrs McDonald's face. 'Class *pet*?'

I didn't like the sound of this. Gamble's not exactly normal. He's small and puny with a little shaved head like a grape, and you never know what he might do next. His favourite hobby is 'headbutting stuff' and he once had to go to hospital after sticking his tongue in a plug socket.

'Thought I should order one, miss,' said Gamble, 'Cos your guinea pigs are a bit boring.'

Mrs McDonald pursed her lips and laid a hand on the guinea pig cage. She *loves* her guinea pigs (Mrs Wiggles and her seven babies) and doesn't like to hear a bad word against them.

'ACCHHOOOO!' sneezed Rosie, showering the back of my head with snot drops. 'We are *not* having any more pets in this room. My therapist says I shouldn't go near any disgusting creatures.'

'Why are you looking at me?' said Gamble, who had just picked his ear and was now sniffing his finger.

'Can't think,' said Rosie flatly, before turning back to Mrs McDonald. 'But ever since *Roman* ruined my life . . .'

'How di—?' I began.

'ACHOO!' she roared, then stood up and began

slapping the table. 'Because of the trauma of . . . what *Roman* made that cow do to me . . . I've become allergic to all furry creatures.'

Mrs McDonald tried to speak but Rosie jabbed a finger towards the cage to cut her off. 'So you'd better get rid of those disgusting rats today or I'll sue the school.'

'I've told you, Rosie,' sighed Mrs McDonald, 'as soon as I find a new babysitter for the piggy wiggies I'll stop br—'

Rosie interrupted her again. 'And *BTW* – which *FYI* is short for *by the way* – if anyone else dares to bring any animals into this classroom, there's a good chance I'll sneeze myself to death. And, if I do, I promise my ghost will haunt you forever.'

She plonked herself down in her chair and angrily folded her arms.

Since the cow had given her a pat on the head, Rosie had sneezed and sniffed at the slightest mention of any animal. Personally I didn't think there was anything wrong with her and she was just doing it for attention.

Mrs McDonald took a deep breath. 'Thank you, Rosie. Now, Darren, what was all this about a class pet?'

Gamble bounced around excitedly in his chair. 'Well, miss. Someone left the school credit card lying around in the office so I thought I'd buy something for the class. Amazing what you can get online.'

'That sounds a bit . . . *illegal*,' said Mrs McDonald. 'What *exactly* did you order?'

'A goat.'

'Phew. I was worried it was something danger—'

'Yeah, miss,' grinned Gamble, 'it came free as food for the tiger.'

'*Tiger?!*'

A few people let out a yelp. Gamble looked around him, his shiny little head twitching. 'Every school needs a tiger, miss. I'm gonna call it Nigel. It can live under my desk. And when it's eaten the goat we can just let it hunt on the field.'

'Hunt *what* exactly?' asked Mrs McDonald, her voice quivering.

Gamble looked at her like she was thick. 'People, of course. Don't worry, miss. You'll be alright. I'll train him to leave you alone cos I love you, miss. And anyway, he'll probably pick off all the weak kids first. Then he'll move on to the fatties. And after that . . .'

As he spoke, people began to panic. Kevin 'Grand Old Puke of York' Harrison clasped his hand over his mouth.

'Don't worry, everyone,' yawned Miss Clegg, 'the order didn't go through. The bank rang the school to ask if they'd meant to spend twenty thousand pounds at *maneatingbeasts dot com*. They cancelled the payment.'

Everyone sighed with relief.

'Aw, what's the point in being here at all?" screeched Gamble, before stomping across the classroom and crawling into the art cupboard under the sink.

This kind of behaviour is normal for Gamble. You could say he has a bit of a temper. Once, we went on a school visit to an art gallery and he punched a hole in one of the paintings because 'the man in it was giving me evils'.

Royal Badgers

'So what was the news, miss?' asked Vanya. As well as being amazing at everything, she likes to ask questions.

'Ah yes. Thank you, Vanya,' said Mrs McDonald.

'I haven't been this excited since Mrs Wiggles got chosen to be in that advert.'

You might have seen this advert when it was on TV last year. It starts with a man sitting on the loo (luckily you can only see his shoulder with the top of the toilet behind him). He reaches out with his hand, searching for the loo roll, but somehow accidentally picks up a fluffy white guinea pig (Mrs Wiggles). The camera points at Mrs Wiggles' face for a moment (the guinea pig manages to look terrified, which is pretty impressive acting for a guinea pig). Then the man moves the guinea pig towards his . . . you know . . . *wiping zone*. The screen goes black just in time and the voiceover says: 'Pupdrex toilet tissue – so soft you could mistake it for anything.'

It's horrible.

'So . . .' said Mrs McDonald, clapping her hands excitedly. 'Before we watch a short film, who can tell me what they think about badgers?'

'Urgh yuck. They're gross,' said Rosie. 'I bet they eat their own poo or something. Bit like Roman . . .'

A couple of people tittered.

'Eh?' I said.

Rosie ignored me. 'And, frankly, black, white and grey together? Boring. It's like, why not accessorise? Try some gold shoes or a red headband or something.'

Typical Rosie.

Mrs McDonald swallowed. 'Well, that's not what I . . .'

'Miss, I love 'em,' said Gamble, climbing out of the cupboard and walking across a couple of tables before dropping down into his chair.

'So nice to see a young animal lover, Darren,' said Mrs McDonald. She has to ignore most of Gamble's bad behaviour, otherwise she wouldn't have time to do anything else.

'They're well cute, miss,' he said.

'Yes they a—'

'And delicious.'

There was a short pause. Mrs McDonald looked like she'd swallowed a coconut. 'I'm sorry, Darren, I thought you just said . . . ahem . . . *delicious*.'

Gamble grinned. 'I did, miss. They taste a bit like ham. Mixed with car bumper. And a little sprinkle of road.'

'Oh.'

'Dad ran one over the other week,' explained Gamble. 'We always eat dead stuff off the road, miss. One time we ate a hitchhiker.'

'*WHAT????*' screamed Mrs McDonald.

'Wouldn't surprise me,' grunted Miss Clegg, who seemed to be playing Candy Crush on her phone under the desk.

Kevin 'Grand Old Puke of York' Harrison stood up, holding his belly. 'Miss, I feel . . .'

'Just go, Kevin,' sighed Mrs McDonald, before turning back to Gamble. 'You *ate* a *hitchhiker*? One of those people who stands by the side of the road asking for a lift?'

Gamble slapped his forehead, spreading out the ink and blood. 'No. Not one of *them*. Silly me. It was a *hedgehog*. Same thing though, innit?'

'Not really.'

'Best thing is, miss,' Gamble went on excitedly, 'if you cut a hedgehog up into little chunks it comes served on its own cocktail sticks.'

Kevin Harrison charged out of the room.

Rosie Taylor sneezed again, this time into my ear. 'See – even *thinking* about animals makes me allergic.'

I wiped it off with my sleeve. 'Thanks for that.'

Vanya tutted at her. 'You could sneeze into your hand like a normal person, you know?'

'Well, Vanya, I know that *you* like hanging

around with crusty little bogies,' said Rosie, glancing at me. 'But I'm not getting mucus on my fingers, thank you. Hashtag – snot gonna happen.'

'And what if Roman gets ill?' said Vanya. She always sticks up for me, which is nice.

Rosie held up her bright red fingernails. 'These fake nails cost twenty-five quid. I really don't think Roman's life is worth that much, do you?'

'Thanks again,' I said.

'Can we **PLEASE** get back to the badgers?' howled Mrs McDonald. 'I have an important announcement to make.'

'Fine, jeez, chill out,' tutted Rosie.

Huffing out her cheeks, Mrs McDonald switched off the lights and we watched a film on the interactive whiteboard. It was all about a badger hospital. There was a badger with a broken leg, an old badger being fitted with false teeth, then a few badgers snuffling round a pen, nudging a football around with their noses. Everyone thought they were really cute – like flat, stumpy, black-and-white bears — and all the girls went *awwwwww* when it showed a woman bottlefeeding milk to a fluffy little baby badger.

Then the camera panned out to reveal that it

wasn't just *any* woman. It was a beautiful young woman with mega-fancy clothes on and perfect hair. Everyone gasped.

Mrs McDonald pressed pause. 'Does anyone know who this is?'

I knew who she was straight away because she is pretty much the most famous person in the whole world. Plus my grandma is obsessed with her and she'd been on about her ever since she'd arrived at our house the day before.

I put my hand up to answer but, before I could say anything, Rosie Taylor was on her feet again.

'OMG! It's Princess Lucy!' she squealed. 'She's going to be the queen one day. She's, like, the most beautiful woman in the world. Stylish. Elegant. Gorgeous.' She paused to run her fingers through her hair. 'Many people have likened her to me actually.'

I tried not to laugh here but I couldn't help it. Rosie Taylor thinks she's AMAZING but really she's got a face like a broken elbow.

'Oh, like you'd know anything about looking good, Roman,' she sneered, jabbing me in the shoulder with one of her razor-sharp nails. 'You're a hideous little gremlin.'

Charming.

Gamble scratched an angry spot on his scalp. 'I proper love the royal family me, but I thought Princess Lucy was that old geezer with the big ears.'

'No, you scummy peasant,' snapped Rosie Taylor, 'that's *Prince* Carl. Princess Lucy is married to his son, Prince Wilfred.'

Mrs McDonald pressed play again and Princess Lucy spoke to the camera in her lovely posh voice. 'Hello. I'm Princess Lucy and I simply adore two things in the world – clothes and badgers.'

Rosie jumped out of her chair. 'Hashtag SNAP! I *LOOOOOOOOVE* badgers too. They're gorgetabulous and cute-amungous. That's another thing I've got in common with the princess.'

'But you just said . . .' I began, turning round to look at her.

Rosie interrupted by sneezing again, this time right in my face. I was beginning to think that she was doing this on purpose.

'So,' continued Princess Lucy on the screen, 'that's why I'm starting a new charity called "Badges for Badgers". You'll be able to buy a badge from any high street clothes shop and your one pound donation will go towards helping sick badgers in animal hospitals all over the country.'

Mrs McDonald stopped the film. She looked so excited I thought she was going to explode. 'And would you like to know the best news?' she said. 'Princess Lucy is launching her campaign in **our town**.'

'*Yesss*,' hissed everyone in the class.

Apart from me, that is, because I already knew this.

'And she's coming **this Friday**.'

'*Yesss*,' hissed everyone for the second time.

Again, apart from me, because I already knew *this* as well. When I said Grandma is obsessed with Princess Lucy, I really meant it. In her house she has a Princess Lucy clock, a Princess Lucy teapot and matching mugs, Princess Lucy bath towels, and a really creepy remote-controlled Princess Lucy robot with glowing eyes.

In fact, this was the whole reason Grandma had come to stay. Because Grandma is a member of the Princess Lucy Official Fan Club, she'd been sent a special exclusive email about the visit before anyone else found out. She'd decided to visit us and spend the week at our house so she could see the princess in the flesh on Friday.

This was all very nice and everything, but I definitely didn't share her excitement. The royal visit was also the reason why she'd given me the horrible woolly jumper. And trust me, I *really* didn't want to be reminded about that.

Mrs McDonald clapped her hands together. 'And even better . . . well. Maybe I should let someone else tell you. . .'

We all looked towards the door.

What Are You Doing Here?

A tall, tanned man strode in. He was wearing an expensive-looking shiny grey suit and sunglasses, even though he was indoors. 'No, YOU listen, you complete moron,' he barked into his mobile phone, holding his finger up to show us that we had to wait. 'I don't care how sick you are. I don't even care if you have to crawl out of the hospital before they've finished the operation then slither to work on your belly. If you want to keep your job you'll be there when I get back. Loser.'

He jabbed his finger at the phone and huffed out his cheeks before flashing a brilliant, white-toothed smile at the class.

Everyone sat there staring at him.

'Wow!' whispered Vanya to me. 'Who's *that* horrible person?'

I kept quiet. I knew exactly who he was.

'Daddy!' squealed Rosie Taylor, leaping to her feet and running to the front.

Vanya shrugged. 'Ah. That explains everything.'

'Honeybunch,' said Rosie's dad, pushing his sunglasses up into his greased-up hair as Rosie threw her arms round him.

After a moment, Rosie pulled away and frowned at him. 'What are you doing here, Daddy? Why didn't you inbox me to tell me you were coming?'

Rosie's dad held out his arms and gave her a grin. 'Surprise! I wanted to tell you about it in person.'

'I hate surprises!' snapped Rosie. 'Except for presents. This'd better be good. Otherwise I'll be cross. And you *don't* want to make me cross, do you, Daddy?'

'No, darling,' gulped Rosie's dad. For such a nasty person, he seemed very scared of Rosie. 'But I really think you might like this.'

She folded her arms and stared at him expectantly. 'Get on with it then.'

'OK,' said Rosie's dad, turning to the class. 'Who knows what I do for a living?'

Nobody put their hands up.

He ground his teeth together and looked at his watch. 'Time is money, people.'

Rosie rolled her eyes and spoke to us like we were two-year-olds. 'He's a VID – a Very Important Daddy. He owns the massive shopping centre in town, which I think you'll find means he's better than any of your parents.'

'Are you sure?' said Vanya coolly. 'Because my dad's a VID too – a Very Important *Doctor*, that is – he works at a hospital for sick children.'

'Huh!' scoffed Rosie. 'Well, my dad's so rich he could *buy* a load of sick children if he wanted to, then put them to work cleaning his shops.'

I felt my mouth dropping open. Even by Rosie's standards, this was pretty low.

Rosie's dad held up his hands and laughed. 'Well. Of course I wouldn't do that,' he said. Then he sniffed. 'Although it *is* true that I probably could.'

Mrs McDonald stepped forward. 'You were going to tell us some news, Mr Taylor.'

'Oh yes,' said Rosie's dad. 'So, you know that there'll be *two* princesses in town on Friday . . .'

He winked at Rosie, who said, 'He means me,'

like we weren't able to figure that out for ourselves. I felt physically sick.

Rosie's dad carried on. 'Well, Her Royal Highness is coming to my shopping centre to launch this squirrel charity thing.'

'It's badgers,' said Vanya.

'Whatever,' said Rosie's dad, waving her away. 'And we thought it'd look good on the photos if we had some kids there and . . . well . . . since my little darling goes to this school . . .'

Mrs McDonald was unable to contain herself any longer. 'WE are going to be greeting the princess when she arrives!'

'YOUMEANI'MGONNAMEETPRINCESS-LUCY!!!' shrieked Rosie, leaping around like she was having a fit.

'That's right, sweetheart. Thought I should tell you all myself. Till old mega-mouth McDonald here ruined it,' he said bitterly. 'First rule of business: never leave big news to the little people.'

He jerked his thumb towards Mrs McDonald, whose face dropped. 'Hang on. What do you mean "little people"?'

'You know,' he replied airily. 'The grunts, the slaves, the drones, the dropouts, the dung beetles. No offence.'

Mrs McDonald looked like he'd caused plenty of offence but before she could say anything, Rosie began yabbering away. 'OMflippingG, Daddy. You're buying me a new outfit. And we're gonna *have* to phone Antonio and get him to style my hair that morning and . . .'

'Anything to make you happy,' her dad smarmed. 'Now I gotta go. Deals to do. People to fire. See you Friday, kids. Mwah.'

With that, he strutted out. Meanwhile, the class reacted like they'd just been told we were going into space. Everyone was cheering and squealing and clapping and high-fiving each other. Rosie had her mobile out and was updating her status on seven different social media platforms. Gamble was so excited he ate a rubber and repeatedly punched himself in the face. Kevin 'Grand Old Puke of York' Harrison, who'd only just made it back into the room, had to rush straight out to hurl again. Even Mrs McDonald seemed to forget she'd just been insulted and did this weird little dance that made her look like a drunk jellyfish. It was pandemonium.

Personally, I had other things on my mind. Through the little window of the classroom door I could see the top of someone's face and head. Someone short with white curly hair. Someone who probably shouldn't have been there.

Grandma.

She noticed me looking and waggled a plastic bag at the little window.

I gulped.

I didn't like the look of this at all.

Enter the Crumper

Now, I love my grandma, like I said. She's sweet and kind and lovely. But that doesn't necessarily mean I want her to come into my classroom. She's a bit, well . . .

'Where is he? Where is he?' she squealed, waddling uninvited into the room like a chubby pink hurricane of lipstick and knitwear. She squinted through her thick glasses, scanning the whole room before finally seeing me. 'Ooh-hoo! There he is! My little Roman soldier! Coo-eee!'

See what I mean?

I shrank down in my seat and waved back with one hand while covering my face with the other. A snigger rippled around the room.

'Classic,' said Rosie smugly.

'Can I help?' asked Mrs McDonald. 'How did you get in here?'

'I followed that nice man in the suit. Just came in to drop this off for Roman,' she said. The bright plastic bangles on her wrist rattled as she held up the bag. 'You forgot to wear the present I gave you, my sweet little coconut.'

I felt my face turning red. 'Whoops.'

'I noticed you didn't have it on when you left home and I thought: "Ooh, he'll be SO upset when he realises he's forgotten it."'

My mouth was as dry as a camel's flip-flop. 'Silly me. Did I leave it somewhere by mistake?'

'Oh yes. I had to look everywhere for it. You'd accidentally left it in that old suitcase on top of the wardrobe.'

'Amazing where these things turn up,' I croaked. By the way, I had also *accidentally* locked the suitcase and *accidentally* hidden the key under my bed.

'Well. No harm done. You can put it on now.'

'I'd love to but it's not uniform.'

'I checked at the office,' smiled Grandma. 'At this school, uniform isn't compulsory. You're allowed to wear anything as long as it's smart. Come on. I knitted it especially.'

Grandma is a knitter. She likes to knit. A lot. She has a special knitting machine and she never stops clacking away on it. I don't want to be horrible but, despite all her practice, she's utterly and completely rubbish. This is partly because she's very short-sighted – even though her glasses are as powerful as microscopes she still can't read the patterns.

At home we have a massive box in the loft that's jam-packed with all the crazy woollen stuff she's made for us down the years – clothes, hats, tea-cosies, socks, you name it. Whenever she comes round we have to dig it all out again and wear it so we don't hurt her feelings. But then she thinks we love it so she just makes more and more. It's impossible.

In the past she's made me all kinds of awful things – a woolly T-shirt with two neck holes because she'd 'got the pattern wrong' (I still had to wear it, though, presumably in case I grew a second head); an orange balaclava with a green bobble that made my head look like a carved pumpkin; socks that were so tight that my toes turned blue; and, worst of all, a pair of knitted boxer shorts. And trust me, warm, itchy wool is not the best material for undies.

But this . . . *thing* she'd made for me was the worst ever.

When I didn't stand up, Grandma's face crumpled slightly. 'You did promise . . .'

I winced. Yes, OK, I *had* promised her I'd wear it to school so maybe this *was* my fault. But I only agreed to wear it because I didn't want to make her feel bad. Plus, as well as the jumper, she'd also brought me a pack of six Squidgy Splodge raspberry jam doughnuts (probably the greatest food known to man), and I'd kind of been distracted.

'Can we see it?' asked Rosie. I could tell from her evil little smile that she knew how bad it was going to be.

'With pleasure!' announced Grandma, opening the bag and triumphantly holding up the jumper. I was worried that everyone would laugh, but actually the reaction was even worse: the room suddenly fell into a long, embarrassed silence. It was like someone had farted in a lift. I put my head in my hands and peeped out from between my fingers.

And why did everyone react like this? Well, this wasn't any old grandma-knitted jumper. It was something much, much worse. It was a special woolly jumper to celebrate the princess's visit.

Mrs McDonald squinted at the offending item of clothing. 'Ahem. Wow. That certainly is a . . . er . . .' she said, taking off her glasses then putting them back on again. '. . . *jumper*.'

Well. Just about, yes.

'Hashtag: yikes,' squealed Rosie Taylor. 'THAT is the cruddiest jumper I've ever seen.'

'Ooh. Thank you very much,' said Grandma, who obviously doesn't know what the word 'cruddiest' means.

'In fact,' sniggered Rosie, 'it's a *crumper*.'

As much as I hate to agree with Rosie, on this occasion she was right. I don't want to be harsh but it really was the cruddiest, crummiest, crustiest crumper of all time.

First of all it was the same yellow-brown colour as cat diarrhoea. Plus the arms were about three times too long. And then there was the picture in the middle. Good grief! Grandma *said* it was Princess Lucy but it looked more like a shaved chimpanzee had fallen out of a tree and landed face first in a plate of spaghetti. The 'princess' had a pink, egg-shaped head. A couple of strands of yellow wool dangled down from the scalp, but the rest of her head was totally bald. Then Grandma had sewn on two massive goggly eyes, a triangular nose and a huge, red grinning mouth with weird, crooked teeth. Strangest of all, the bottom half of the princess's face was orange.

Rosie noticed this straight away. 'I particularly like the detail on the ginger beard.'

'Oh, I ran out of pink wool,' smiled Grandma.

'I don't get it,' said Gamble, confused. 'Why have you knitted a massive potato on the front of a sweater?'

'Silly Darren,' said Mrs McDonald, trying to smile. 'That's a person.' She lowered her voice and turned to me. 'Ahem . . . *isn't it*?'

I nodded grimly. 'It's Princess Lucy, isn't it, Grandma?'

'What's with the masher then?' asked Gamble, frowning.

'It's a crown,' said Grandma. 'You'll see when he's wearing it. Come on, Roman, model it for us.'

My eyes nearly popped out of my head. Everyone swivelled round to face me. 'You don't have to do it, Roman,' whispered Vanya.

But the rest of the class didn't agree. Led by Rosie, they began to chant: 'Wear it. Wear it. Wear it.'

Oh, Rosie Taylor was loving this.

'Please no,' I said, shaking my head.

'Why won't you wear it, Roman?' said Rosie, a cruel, mocking smile on her lips. 'Your grandma worked sooooo hard on it.'

I cleared my throat and scratched my neck. 'Well, I thought I could wait until later.'

You know, like, fifty or sixty years later, perhaps?

Grandma's face dropped. She looked really hurt. 'You . . . don't like it, do you?'

'Course he does,' said Mrs McDonald quickly. 'Don't you, Roman?'

'Course I do,' I said, the words hurting my throat as they came out. I couldn't bear to upset Grandma, but maybe Vanya was right – maybe if I stood my ground I wouldn't have to put it on.

Sadly, this possibility didn't last for long.

'Look,' said Grandma. She looked like she was about to cry and she was holding up her hand. Two of her fingers were bandaged together. 'I mangled them in the knitting machine trying to make it perfect.'

I'd already seen this injury the day before but it still made me feel extremely guilty.

'Why are you being so heartless, Roman?' said Rosie, pretending to look horrified. 'How could you refuse to wear that beautiful crumper after your poor grandma risked her life to make it for you?'

A few people shook their heads and tutted.

This was all too much to bear. I kicked back my chair and dragged my feet to the front.

It was no surprise to me that the crumper looked even worse on than it did off, but I think it was a bit of a shock for everyone else. It was so big and baggy that the sleeves practically dragged along the ground. I looked like an orang-utan. Despite this, the neck hole was so tight I thought I might pass out. But, worst of all, the stitching on the princess's face had been pulled so tight that her eyes stuck out in little cones. It looked like I had – you know – *boobs*.

Apart from Vanya and Grandma, everybody in the room cracked up laughing at me.

'Hubba hubba!' said Grandma. 'The girls will go bananas for you.'

'That is the best thing I've ever seen!' howled Rosie Taylor, wiping the tears of laughter from her eyes and taking a snap of me wearing the crumper on her mobile phone. I'd never seen her looking so happy. 'Nice knockers!'

My cheeks were so hot you could've fried an egg on them. I scuttled back to my place and sank back into my seat.

Fundraising

After Grandma had gone – blowing kisses at me as she left – and the laughter had died down, Mrs McDonald told us more about the royal visit. 'We'll all be there in the crowd to see the princess, and three lucky children will actually get to meet her and give her some flowers.'

'Why only three?' asked Vanya.

Mrs McDonald looked a bit awkward. 'Ahem. Rosie's dad didn't want too many. The TV and newspaper people will be there filming and taking photos. He thought you might block out the name of the shopping centre if you were all standing out front when she arrives.'

There's a surprise.

'Well, obviously if there are paparazzi there, *I'll* be meeting her,' said Rosie. 'I've done modelling before.'

Technically this was true. You couldn't see her

face in the photos, though – she was actually modelling a Halloween mask for the Argos catalogue. I'm saying nothing.

'Yes . . . but . . .' began Mrs McDonald.

Rosie cut her off. 'No offence, but everyone else here is a bit . . . well . . . *truglier* than me.'

'Truglier?' asked Mrs McDonald.

'Trampier and uglier,' replied Rosie matter-of-factly.

'That's not very nice, Rosie,' Mrs McDonald said.

'Oh, come on, miss,' said Rosie, flicking back her hair. 'If you were entering one of your guinea pigs for a competition, you wouldn't choose the cross-eyed one with the strange teeth, would you?'

Mrs McDonald spluttered. 'I suppose not, but . . .'

'Or the smelly one with the disgusting habits?'

'Why are you looking at me again?' asked Gamble, scratching his bottom with a pencil.

Rosie held out her arms. 'So it's obvious. Hashtag: pick the pretty one.'

'Well, yes,' said Mrs McDonald, 'it *could* be you, Rosie . . .'

'Obvs,' said Rosie.

'Or . . .' carried on Mrs McDonald, 'It *could* be Vanya, or Roman or . . .'

'What?' shrieked Rosie, pointing at me. 'That vile mutant? Look at his clothes!'

'Even Roman's better than *him*, though,' said Miss Clegg, jerking her thumb at Gamble. 'Darren's not going near her unless he's wearing a choke-lead and a muzzle.'

'Oi! I'm a good boy, me,' said Gamble. But then he kind of ruined things by adding: 'So shut your cakehole, you big whale.'

Mrs McDonald pursed her lips. 'I will be deciding fairly and squarely who is chosen. We're going to try to raise money for the princess's new charity this week. The three people who raise the most will get to meet her. You can work on your own or in groups. There's no time to lose, so let's get planning!'

The class let out a great big *Yessssssss*.

I wrestled off the crumper and put it on the back of my chair.

'This is going to be amazing!' said Vanya, clapping her hands together. 'Let's be partners. We can do *so* much for these poor badgers. And imagine how cool it'd be to actually meet Princess Lucy together.'

I shrugged. I didn't feel as excited as Vanya. I mean, of course I wanted to help the badgers, and I do like working with Vanya. And I wouldn't have *minded* meeting the princess. But I don't really enjoy being the centre of attention. Plus, the crumper had kind of put me off Princess Lucy a little bit.

Completely uninvited, Gamble plonked himself down on our table. 'I'm working with you two.'

Vanya winced. 'Oh great.'

She puts up with Gamble because he's my sort-of friend. She's not his biggest fan, though, ever since he borrowed her gel pens without asking then used them to personalise his underpants.

Gamble didn't notice her sarcasm. 'I know, brilliant, innit?'

I forced a smile.

For the rest of the morning we planned our fundraising ideas. Personally I think that this was just something to keep us busy while Miss Clegg and Mrs McDonald sat at the front and shopped online for clothes to wear for the royal visit.

'If there are three of us, the money's going to be shared out so we need to raise loads,' said Vanya. 'We can't miss out on this. And we definitely can't lose to Rosie. She'd be unbearable.'

Even though I wasn't that bothered, I could see it meant a lot to Vanya. I was determined to at least help *her* to meet Princess Lucy.

'Right,' said Gamble, 'when you need cash fast, the best thing to do is rob it from a bank or a shop.'

Vanya ignored him. 'How about a cake sale?'

'Or a doughnut sale?' I suggested, perking up.

'My brother Spud works at a bakery,' said Gamble. 'I bet he'll get 'em for us. I'll ask him tonight.'

While this conversation was going on, I had to ignore Rosie, who kept on poking me in the shoulder blades and making 'hilarious' remarks about the crumper.

e.g.

'Psst, Roman. Nice pullover. You should <u>pull</u> it <u>over</u> your mingtabulous face.'

'Don't worry, Roman. I can think of two accessories to improve that crumper. Some petrol and a match.'

'I don't do violence, Roman. But, if *I* was wearing *that*, I think I'd beat *myself* up.'

'Hey, Roman – is that a jumper or did Kevin Harrison swallow a ball of wool then throw up on you?'

etc.

Ha. Ha. Ha.

After a while, these comments started to get in the way of our planning.

Vanya turned round and snarled at her. 'Rosie. If you don't leave him alone I'll hit you so hard your nose will be sticking out the back of your skull.'

By the way, Vanya is a black belt in karate. Rosie's bottom lip began to wobble and she thrust her hand in the air. 'Miss! Help! Vanya's being horrible.'

Mrs McDonald didn't look up from her computer. 'That's nice, Rosie,' she said, before carrying on talking to Miss Clegg. 'Well, I *love* the blue dress but I'm worried it'll make my bottom look big.'

'Why don't you come up with your own ideas and stop being so horrible?' I said to Rosie.

Rosie gave a slimy, evil smile, like a man-eating slug. 'Oh, I already have.' She clicked her fingers. 'Mrs McDonald!'

Mrs McDonald was still talking to Miss Clegg: 'No no no. If you wear the red one you'll look like a postbox.'

'MRS MCDONALD!' bellowed Rosie. 'Jeez. Look at me when I'm talking to you.'

Mrs McDonald raised an eyebrow and pursed her lips. 'Yes . . .'

'I've got a plan. We should have a non-uniform day tomorrow.'

'Oh, wonderful,' said Mrs McDonald, clapping her hands together. 'Pay a pound. Wear your own clothes. Let's do it!'

Everyone chattered excitedly. Apart from me, of course. I knew exactly what Rosie was going to say next.

She kept her eyes firmly fixed on me. 'Roman. You should wear that gorgeous crumper.'

'Why would I?'

'So you'll look like an idiot, of course,' she replied, under her breath.

'Definitely not.'

'I thought you'd say that,' said Rosie. Her voice was slow and dangerous. 'So I'm going to sponsor you to do something.' She dialled a number on her phone. Mrs McDonald tried to stop her but Rosie waved her away. 'Oh, hello, Daddykins,' she began in a horrible baby voice, loud enough for the whole class to hear. 'You'll do a teeny-weeny favour for your icky-wicky princess, won't you? I need to sponsor a boy in my class to do something. Just a hundred pounds should do it.'

A hundred quid!

'Well, OK, let's make it two hundred since you love me so much. Thank you. Love you too. Mwah. Mwah.'

She hung up and her face hardened. 'Sucker,' she said, before turning to me. 'All settled then, Roman. You're locked in.'

There was no need for her to tell me what she was sponsoring me to do because I knew already. I glared at her. 'I'm not doing it.'

Rosie brushed a strand of hair out of her eyes. 'All the money can go to Badges for Badgers. Think of how many sick and injured little creatures you'll be able to save.'

'That *would* be pretty cool,' said Vanya to me.

'Oh, how generous, Rosie. And what will he have to do?' asked Mrs McDonald innocently. I said nothing.

Rosie licked her lips. 'All he has to do is wear his crumper . . . all week.'

A whole week? That's almost a thousand years. 'Not a chance.'

'Ommmm!' exclaimed Rosie, putting her hand

in front of her mouth in disbelief. 'Roman's trying to kill badgers again.'

'What do you mean, *again*?'

'Face it,' said Rosie, 'it's the kind of thing you do.'

I was starting to get pretty fed up. 'I don't think it is.'

'Well, Roman, it doesn't seem like much to ask,' said Mrs McDonald. 'It's for such a good cause.'

'But I don't want to w—'

'Badger murderer!' snapped Rosie.

A couple of people gasped like this was actually true.

'What?' I said. 'You can't honestly think I'd . . .'

But my voice trailed away. Half the class was staring like they'd just walked in on me kicking a sackful of baby badgers or something.

'I didn't know you were so cruel,' said Gamble, which was a bit rich coming from him. His idea of being kind is to stop wedgying you when you go unconscious.

'My daddy will destroy you in court if you don't do it,' warned Rosie. 'Breaking a promise *and* massacring badgers? They'll probably bring back the death penalty just for you.'

'That's crackers,' I said.

Rosie sniffed. 'Well, maybe. But he could still sue you. And, hang on . . .' A smile spread across her face. 'I've seen you outside the Squidgy Splodge doughnut shop at Daddy's shopping centre before, licking the glass like a hungry rat.'

The mention of the shop instantly made my tummy rumble. It is the biggest Squidgy Splodge outlet in the whole country – and probably the greatest place in the whole world – rack upon rack of beautiful, plump, sweet balls of heaven. 'What about it?'

'One phone call to Daddy and you'll be banned from there for life.'

'You wouldn't!' I gasped. If there's one thing Rosie knows, it's how to find your weak spot. She might as well have threatened to ban me from breathing.

Rosie waved her phone at me and smiled cruelly. 'Try me.'

'I know she's horrible, Roman, and the jumper is a bit embarrassing, but you *would* be doing a lot for the badgers,' said Vanya.

I gulped. The last thing I wanted to do was let Vanya down. Well, obviously, by that I mean the last thing *after* being banned from the Squidgy Splodge shop.

'Oh come on, Roman,' said Mrs McDonald. 'You can do it!'

The class began to chant at me again. 'Do it! Do it!'

'Can't ignore popular opinion,' said Miss Clegg, like it had anything to do with her.

It seemed like I had no choice. At least I'd be helping the badgers. And it would make Vanya and Grandma happy. I sighed wearily and yanked the crumper back on over my head. 'Fine.'

Rosie leaned back in her chair and clapped. 'Brilliant.'

After School

When the Crumper Caused an Accident and Gave Me a Blocked Nose

At the end of school, I set off home with Gamble and Vanya, munching sadly on my last doughnut. Things weren't looking good on the fundraising front. Because we were in a group of three, it meant our money would have to be divided three ways. We'd have to raise tonnes to be allowed to meet the princess. Rosie had already made sure that the money from the non-uniform day *and* from my sponsored crumper-wearing would go to her total. I didn't think this was fair – especially the sponsored crumper-wearing, when I'd be suffering for it – but there was nothing I could do. Rosie had argued with Mrs McDonald that there wouldn't be a royal visit in the first place if it wasn't for her dad. And, after her interruptions, my group hadn't had a single other fundraising idea. We were starting to get a bit desperate.

'The doughnut sale's a good start,' said Vanya, 'but we're going to need more ways of raising money.'

'Bras,' said Gamble.

'What?' I asked.

Gamble shrugged. 'All women need 'em. So we'll nick a load off washing lines then sell 'em on.'

Unbelievable. Who on earth would buy stolen secondhand bras off Gamble?

'Roman. Remind me why you're friends with him?' said Vanya, sounding seriously cheesed off.

I couldn't really answer that. I had bigger things to worry about – like the crumper. Unfortunately, Rosie Taylor was following a hundred metres behind to make sure I didn't take it off. We were about halfway home, just coming up to the canal bridge. After the bridge we usually split up: Gamble turns left, Vanya goes right and I carry straight on. When none of us could come up with another fundraising idea, the conversation moved on to the royal visit.

'I hope we get to meet her,' said Gamble. 'I'm

gonna give the princess a right big kiss on the lips and maybe she'll take me back to the palace with her and I can live there forever and be her maid.'

'Hmmm . . .' said Vanya. 'I'm not sure that's going to happ—'

She was interrupted by Gamble pointing in front of us and shrieking, 'Hey, it's Spud! I'll ask him about the doughnuts!'

We looked up. About fifty metres in front of us, a motorcycle was weaving across the canal bridge. The rider wasn't wearing a helmet, and he wasn't watching where he was going either. In fact, he was steering with one hand while tipping a large bag of cheesy Wotsits into his mouth with the other. And this wasn't even the most dangerous thing. What looked like an enormous plastic wheel was propped up next to him on the motorbike. It was balanced precariously on the edge of the seat, with his steering arm threaded through between the spokes. It looked like it could roll off at any second.

I'd never met Gamble's brother Spud before but, as he got closer, I could see that he looked exactly like a bigger version of Darren – the same bald baked-bean head and the same scrawny arms poking out of a ripped T-shirt.

'Alright, Spud!' yelled Darren, as the motorbike came within ten metres of us.

In the space of a few seconds, several things happened almost at once.

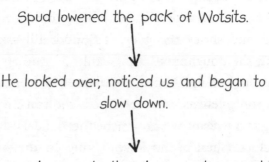

Spud lowered the pack of Wotsits.

He looked over, noticed us and began to slow down.

A massive gap-tooth grin spread across his face. At first I thought that this was because he'd seen Darren. But then . . .

. . . he lifted his hand off the handlebar so he could point at me.

It was at that moment that I realised that Spud Gamble isn't exactly the cleverest person on the planet. Now I'm no expert, but I'm pretty sure you need at least one hand on the handlebars to steer a motorbike.

'HA!' he cried. 'What a rubbish jum—'

He didn't finish. Suddenly the massive cartwheel-thing tipped to one side, causing the motorbike to swing out of control. Spud made a grab for the handlebar but it was too late. The front of the bike crunched into the kerb, catapulting him forward. We dived out of the way as Spud flew over the handlebars, turned a somersault in mid-air and slammed face first onto someone's front garden in a shower of cheesy Wotsits. The big wheel trundled along the pavement and crashed into a bus shelter.

Vanya, Gamble and I were lying on the tarmac in a tangled heap, with the motorbike on its side just in front of us. The front forks were slightly twisted and its buckled wheel was slowly spinning round. The engine spluttered a few times then died.

I gulped.

The crumper had caused a road accident.

But things were about to get worse.

Surprise Attack

As I lay in a daze, staring at the motorbike, I felt two hands grabbing me from behind and spinning me round. *Spud*. He looked seriously angry. Before

I could say anything, he'd shoved a cheesy Wotsit up each of my nostrils.

'Yooooww!' I screamed. 'Bhat bas bat bor?'

'Leave him alone!' snapped Vanya. 'That was your fault.'

'Don't think so!' said Spud, dragging me to my feet and jabbing me in the chest with a bony finger. 'As if you walk down the street wearin' a jumper like that? Course I'm gonna be distracted. I could've been killed!'

I didn't think it was the right time to tell him that riding a motorbike no-handed wasn't exactly a good idea. I decided to take the blame and hope he didn't attack me with any more salty snacks. 'Borry about your botorbike,' I snuffled, finding it difficult to breathe.

'You can let him go,' said Gamble, getting to his feet. 'He's alright.'

Spud huffed out his cheeks and shoved me backwards then turned to his brother. 'Darren,' he said, 'you need to choose your mates better. This one'll get you into trouble.'

I would've laughed if I could've breathed properly. Instead I massaged my throat and snorted the Wotsits out of my nose.

Spud walked over to the big wheel thing, leaned it against the bus shelter and started inspecting it. It was about as tall as me and it was made of bulky black plastic. There were six sturdy spokes inside the wheel and eight or nine little helicopter propellers around the outside of it.

Spud lifted it off the ground and flicked a switch underneath. The propellers began to spin round. Then he placed it flat on the ground, pulled his mobile phone out of his pocket and started swiping his fingers around the screen. The wheel-thing slowly took off and hovered about six feet in the air.

'Cool!' I said, almost forgetting what had just happened to my nose. 'Is that a drone?'

Spud sniffed, slowly lowering it back to earth. It landed softly on the ground and he switched it off. 'Not just any drone – this is the Eagle Smash Gyrocopter 3000. It can carry twenty kilos and fly over thirty miles. It's got an HD video camera that could film a flea up close from two miles away.'

'It's well good, innit?' grinned Darren.

'There's only ten in the whole country,' said Spud, proudly.

'And where did *you* get it?' asked Vanya, unimpressed.

'Pinched it from the back of an army lorry,' Spud said. His voice was casual, as though he'd just said 'I bought it at Tesco'. 'It's worth ten thousand quid. So if you *had* smashed it, I'd have pulled off your butt cheeks and made you eat 'em.'

'He's done that before,' warned Gamble.

'Good to know,' I squeaked. I wasn't sure exactly how that would work but it sounded pretty painful.

'You touch his buttocks and I'll snap your wrist off,' growled Vanya.

This conversation was getting a bit violent and a bit too much about my buttocks for my liking, but I was glad Vanya was on my side. Even though she was half his size and five years younger, she faced up to Spud in a karate stance, fists up. Spud squinted at her for a moment, then smiled and turned away. 'Alright. Relax. I ain't got time to smash your chops in. I'm on my way to visit Uncle Terry in prison before my night shift at work. I'm gonna fly the drone over the prison walls and drop him in some sausage rolls from the bakery and a few bum-worm tablets. Uncle Terry can't get either of 'em in jail.'

I've met Gamble's uncle Terry before. He accidentally kidnapped me once when he'd just broken into our local shop. He and Scratchy (Gamble's pet dog) both suffer from worms. I've no idea who caught them off who.

'Can you pinch us some doughnuts tonight from work?' asked Darren.

Spud spat on the ground. 'Alright. But I ain't doing it for free. Look at my motorbike.'

'What do you want?'

Slowly, Spud turned to face me. 'How about you give us that rubbish jumper?'

I looked around. 'What? This one?'

'Course that one. Can't see any others. I can put the stuff for Uncle Terry in it, like a really bad carrier bag.'

Wow. You know your jumper's awful when someone suggests using it to wrap up stolen sausage rolls and bum-worm tablets.

'Don't give it to him,' said Vanya.

As much as I wanted to get rid of the crumper, I couldn't risk making Rosie mad.

'The thing is,' I said to Spud, 'my grandma made it and I don't want to hurt her feelings and I've kind of been sponsored to wear it and . . .'

Before I could finish though, Spud had pulled it up over my head and was yanking it off my arms.

With one final violent heave, my head had popped through the tight neck hole.

'Hey! Give that back!' snarled Vanya, but Spud pushed her away and started controlling the drone with his phone again. It lifted up and hovered in the air again, directly in front of him. Then he tapped the screen of his phone. A tiny trapdoor under the drone opened up and a robotic arm with a pincer on the end emerged. Spud held the crumper under it and tapped his screen again with his thumb. The pincer grabbed the crumper and the drone rose higher in the air.

'How good is that?' he said.

Under normal circumstances, I might've said 'very'. But these were not normal circumstances.

About fifty metres away, Rosie Taylor was striding towards us. I needed to get the crumper back pronto. I jumped up to grab it but Spud flicked it up just out of my reach.

'Come on, let him have it back,' said Vanya. Rosie was now twenty metres away. I could tell by the way she was speeding up that she'd noticed that I wasn't wearing the crumper.

'Alright, alright,' said Spud, 'I'm just messing.'

He lowered the drone so that the crumper was

dangling right above my head. I reached out for it but, just as I was about to grab it, the drone shot forward.

Spud bent double with laughter. 'Unlucky! You'll have to do better than that!'

And so I became the first person in history to run down a street chasing a rubbish jumper that was hanging underneath a military drone. It was *so* frustrating. Every time I got near it, it would zip out of my grasp again, accompanied by howls of laughter from Spud and Darren.

Finally, completely breathless, I reached the canal bridge. The drone was hovering above the water, level with my head but just beyond my reach. I leaned against the wall and turned back towards Spud, panting. 'Please let me have it!'

'Alright, keep your willy on,' he sniggered. 'I was just messing with you, innit. Can't wait to take the camera off the drone and see the film of this.'

He inched the drone towards me. But then, just as I thought he was going to give it to me, he did something really bad. The arms of the pincer opened and the crumper dropped, floating past me and down towards the canal path.

'Whoops! Wrong button!'

I didn't have time to be cross or upset though, because there was a sudden yell from somewhere beneath me. 'Aaaaarrrrgh! Gerrit off meee!'

Swans and Maggots

I peered over the wall of the bridge. 'Oh doughnuts!' I said.

About ten feet below, there was a fisherman lying on his back on the canal towpath. His stool had flipped over, his net and rod were pointing upwards, and all his boxes were scattered around him. His legs were wriggling in the air like an upturned beetle and he was desperately wrestling the crumper off his face.

'I'm being attacked! Help! Call the police!' he screamed, flailing his arms around.

I darted down the stone steps by the side of the bridge and reached the bottom just as he pulled the crumper off his face and flung it onto the towpath. The fisherman struggled to his feet, grabbed the crumper and thrust it towards me in a clenched fist. 'Are you trying to kill me? What do you call this?'

'It's a jumper,' I said.

This was the wrong thing to say. 'I can see that now!' he snapped. 'But it could've been anything! What was it doing on my head?' Although he was quite a fat man, his voice was high-pitched like a cat being ironed. His face was bright purple and there were flecks of spit caught in his beard.

I opened my mouth to explain but the man carried on ranting. 'I've been ill for months. Stressed out. High blood pressure. My doctor said I should take up fishing to calm me down. You could've given me a heart attack. I thought I was being attacked by a giant bat. And look at all my bait. It's everywhere.'

I looked down and immediately jumped backwards. The boxes he'd tipped over had been full of maggots. Millions of them. Horrible, wriggly, nasty little grubs that were now squirming all over the path. I kicked a couple of them off my shoes. When I looked back up, I noticed them all over the crumper as well, crawling in and out of the stitches and wiggling across Princess Lucy's knitted face. Up until that moment, I hadn't thought that anything could've made the crumper worse.

'I'm so sorry,' I began, 'but please may I have my jumper b—'

The man shoved the crumper in my face, showering me with maggots. 'Oh, so *now* you want your jumper back, do you? This one that nearly murdered me?'

Before I could come up with an answer, he'd rolled it up into a ball and thrown it right across the canal. It landed on some reeds on the far side.

My heart sank.

'Get it then,' he said, dusting off his hands then crouching down to gather up his maggots. 'Now, come to Daddy, my little beauties . . .'

This was awful. How was I going to get it back? There was no path on the far side of the canal, just a wall about twenty feet high. The canal was about ten metres wide, and I'm as good at swimming as a tortoise tied to a brick. And in any case, the water was the colour of gravy and it absolutely stank. You'd have to be a complete maniac to swim in it.

Speaking of which . . .

At that moment there was a scream from above me on the canal bridge. 'Dive bomb!!!!!'

I looked up. Darren Gamble was standing on top of the bridge wall.

'No!' I yelled. 'Don't do it!'

It was too late.

With a massive Tarzan yell, Gamble leapt into the air. He seemed to hang there for a moment before plummeting downwards, arms windmilling, then plunging into the murky water with an enormous splash. My mouth fell open. Had he any idea how dangerous that was? The kid is utterly deranged.

A cloud of bubbles rose to the surface.

Then nothing.

Up on the bridge, Vanya was staring down, horrified. We looked at each other for a moment then back at the water.

Where was he?

Just as I was starting to worry Gamble wasn't coming back, he burst up out of the water like a disgusting dolphin. 'I touched the bottom!' he yelled. 'It was well good – there was a shopping trolley down there!'

He swam raggedly across the canal then held onto the wall while untangling the crumper from the reeds.

'Be careful,' I called.

'Yeah, whatever, Mum,' replied Gamble, glancing over at me as he gave the crumper one last tug.

But, just as his head was turned, something

emerged from the reeds. Something huge and white and covered in feathers.

'SWAN!' I yelled.

Have you ever seen an angry swan? They're terrifying! The murderous black eyes, the deadly orange beak, the evil little head. It let out a fierce *hisss* and drew back its long white neck.

'Swim for your life!' I yelled, but Gamble wasn't scared in the slightest bit.

'Fancy some, do ya?' he snarled, swiping a wild punch at it.

Honestly. What kind of a crazy loon tries to thump a swan?

The swan weaved out of the way then its head shot forward like a cobra. Gamble ducked under the water then kicked up again and grabbed it by the wing. The swan cried out in panic and flapped desperately to escape.

Then Gamble did something awful. And I mean *truly awful*.

He bit the swan.

I'm not joking: I saw him clamp his mouth shut around its wing, like it was a big feathery slice of pizza. The swan let out an even louder screech and thrashed itself free before flapping off along the canal.

'Yeah! That's it! Run away, you coward!' screamed Gamble, splashing water after it.

'Good grief,' said Vanya, who'd come down the steps and was standing next to me. 'Did I just see him *bite* that swan?'

I couldn't find the words to reply. This was easily the worst thing I'd ever seen Gamble do. Even worse than the time he played 'Human Ten-pin Bowling' with those Reception class kids and that giant exercise ball. My mouth gaping open, I watched as Gamble swam back to land, holding the crumper in the air above him. When he reached the side he grabbed onto the grassy bank, hauled himself out and spat some water onto the ground. 'Nice one. I won't need to have a bath this week now.'

'Right . . .' I said, stepping away from him. I hoped he was joking. He smelled like an old toilet.

'I've kept the jumper dry,' he grinned, 'but my clothes are proper soaked.'

Before I could stop him, he'd whipped off his uniform so he was standing there on the canal bank in just his underpants. And trust me, this wasn't something I wanted to look at.

'Gross,' said Vanya, turning away.

As I stood there speechless, Gamble wrung out

his clothes and dried himself all over – *and yes, I mean* **all** *over* – with the crumper. Then he held it out to me. ''Ere you go, mate. Glad I kept it dry. Cheers for that.'

I stared at it. It was crawling with maggots, soaked with smelly canal water and, worst of all, it had been wiped across Gamble's most revolting regions.

'You know what,' I said, holding up my hands, 'I think I'm OK for jumpers right now.'

Gamble pulled some slimy pond weed off his skinhead. 'But I risked my life . . .'

'And you've been sponsored, Roman,' said Rosie Taylor from up on the canal bridge.

There was a horrible, smarmy sneer across her slug's bum mouth. She must've seen the whole thing.

'Wait a minute . . .' I said.

Rosie narrowed her eyes. 'You wouldn't want me to tell Daddy, would you, Roman? He's a very rich, powerful man. He'll have you locked up, and even when you get out you won't be allowed within ten miles of his Squidgy Splodge shop. Not to mention your poor old grandma – she'd be heartbroken if she found out you weren't wearing it.'

I gulped. 'But . . .'

'NOW!' she snarled. 'Or I'll even take a photo

and show it to the princess on Friday. When she finds out how you've cheated her charity she'll probably have you beheaded.'

'You'd better put it on,' said Gamble. 'It's a bit cruel on the badgers if you don't.'

This was a bit rich coming from a kid who'd just munched on a live swan.

'You can always take it off again when she's gone,' whispered Vanya.

There was nothing else for it. Very slowly, I pulled the maggot-infested, canal-contaminated, Gamble-ised crumper down over my head.

'That's better. And don't you dare let me catch you without it again,' said Rosie. Just then, a brand new black Range Rover with dark windows pulled up alongside her. 'Oooh, Daddy's here. He's taking me to see my personal stylist, Antonio. I'm having a consultation about how I'm going to have my hair on Friday, since you ask.'

'We didn't,' said Vanya, as Rosie opened the door and hopped into the car.

Once the car had driven off, I turned back to Gamble. He was getting himself dressed again but his clothes were soaked and his scrawny little body was shaking uncontrollably. This wasn't good.

I ran up the steps to check that Rosie was out of sight then came back down and handed Gamble the crumper. Even though he'd just done the cruellest thing I'd ever seen, I didn't want him to catch hypothermia. Plus it was a good excuse for getting rid of it again.

'Ch-ch-cheers, m-m-mate,' he said, teeth chattering and lips pretty much blue. 'B-but I don't want to l-look like an idiot.'

Yep – the crumper was so bad Gamble would genuinely rather have frozen to death than have worn it.

'Just put it on,' snapped Vanya, shoving it over his head.

Gamble shivered again. 'OK. As long as no one sees me. I'll g-give it back tomorrow.'

'You've got to. Otherwise I'll be in mega-trouble,' I said, then looked him up and down. 'And maybe you should wash it as well.'

As we sloshed up the steps, I was so busy brushing maggots off Gamble's back that I barely noticed the fisherman calling someone on his mobile phone.

Unfortunately this phone call was another tangled knot that the crumper was about to tie into the fabric of my life.

TUESDAY

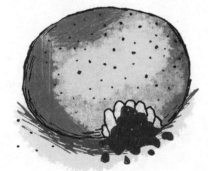

Morning

When Gamble Created a Doughnut Surprise and Gave the Crumper a Wash

When I'd arrived home on Monday night, Grandma had been totally heartbroken that I wasn't wearing the crumper. But she cheered up a lot when I told her that it had prevented Gamble from dying.

'Oooh! I told you it was a special sweater,' she said. 'It even saves lives. Make sure you get it back, mind. He might want to keep it.'

'Hmm,' I said. *I think we'll be alright there.* 'Don't worry, Grandma, I will, I want to wear it tomorrow.'

I decided not to tell her that this was only because I was being sponsored and threatened. It would've just made her upset. Plus, she was so pleased about me wearing it that she gave me another two Squidgy Splodge doughnuts.

The next morning, of course, Rosie Taylor noticed I wasn't wearing the crumper as soon as I reached the playground.

'Where is it?' she growled, striding over to me.

I'd forgotten that today was Wear Your Own Clothes day. She was wearing pink, billowy trousers, a baggy white shirt and a red scarf round her head. She also had a chunky gold earring in her left ear and a diamond-studded eye patch over one eye. In short, she looked ridiculous.

'Gamble needed it,' I said. 'He was freezing. Soon as I see him I'll get it back.'

'Two minutes max,' she said, 'or I swear my dad will have you put in front of a firing squad.'

'Give him a break,' said Vanya, appearing next to me. It was so nice to have a friend who stuck up for me.

Rosie looked Vanya up and down, like she was inspecting a mouldy kebab on a spit. 'Urgh. What *are* you wearing, Vanya?'

'Clothes,' said Vanya, who was wearing an England football shirt and a pair of jeans. She's a bit of a tomboy.

'Well, I hope you're not expecting to meet the princess on Friday dressed like *that*,' said Rosie, pursing her lips. 'She'll think you look like Wayne Goony.'

'Rooney,' said Vanya flatly. 'And at least I'm not dressed like Long John Silver.'

Rosie rolled her eyes. 'You know nothing. Pirate-style is sooo on-trend this season. That American actress Alicia Trogg even cut off her own foot so she could wear a wooden leg.'

'Well, she's an idiot,' said Vanya. 'And anyway – Gamble's over there so Roman can get the jumper back. You can leave us alone now.'

Darren Gamble was by a bench with his back to us. A small circle of people were standing around him, looking at something on the bench. As I got closer, there was a whiff of a familiar smell. A delicious, sweet, perfect smell that clutched me by the belly and pulled me towards it like a big tasty magnet.

Ignoring everything else, I felt my steps quickening and my mouth watering. When I reached the group of people I pushed my way through them and . . . *oh my word*.

I had never seen anything so beautiful in my entire life.

Surprise

Sitting on top of a huge silver plate on the bench was a jam doughnut. And not just any doughnut either. It was the biggest doughnut I've ever seen – easily two feet across – and it was *glorious*: a huge thick pillow of doughy loveliness. The sugar crystals on top glistened in the morning sunlight like tiny diamonds. A thick stream of sweet, succulent jam oozed from the side.

I leaned forward, tongue out, ready to lick it.

'Not so fast!' cried Gamble, pulling me back and pointing to a sign by the side of it. The sign was written in Gamble's scruffy handwriting on a piece of creased paper:

> Big dunot. 10p a bit. Surpriz
> for sum1 in it, innit.

'Good or what?' he grinned. 'It's to raise money for them badgers so we can meet old princess whatserchops.'

Vanya looked impressed with the doughnut. 'Where did you get it?'

'After our Spud had been to see Uncle Terry he

went to work at the bakery,' said Gamble proudly. 'He felt bad about shoving those Wotsits up Roman's nose and there was a load of leftover batter so he made this for us.'

'It's the most gorgeous thing in the world,' I sighed. I genuinely felt close to tears.

Vanya didn't look quite so impressed. 'Well, it's a start, but I reckon you should charge more than ten pence. It's never going to raise enough money to get us to meet the princess. And anyway, where's Roman's jumper?'

I was glad she asked this – I was so mesmerised by the giant doughnut I'd forgotten all about it.

'Relax. I'll make us loads of cash,' said Gamble. Before Vanya could respond, he held up his hand. 'Hold on. Customer.'

Kevin 'Grand Old Puke of York' Harrison held out ten pence to Gamble. 'What's the surprise?'

''Ave a bite and see,' said Gamble, pocketing the money. 'If you pull it out with your teeth you win.'

Kevin leaned forward with his mouth open. He was inches away when Gamble suddenly grabbed the back of his head and plunged it deep into the doughnut. It swallowed his whole head up like a massive yummy helmet.

Vanya tutted. 'Well, that's no good. No one else is going to want a slice now.'

Ignoring her, Gamble dragged Kevin's head out again. His face and hair were completely covered in dough and jam, and he was holding the end of something large and floppy in his teeth.

He spat it out and wiped his sticky face. 'I got it! I got it! What do I win?'

The floppy thing was soaked with jam and still mainly inside the doughnut, so it was hard to say exactly what it was at first – a bin bag? A bed sheet? The skin off a giant rice pudding?

It was only when Gamble yanked all of it out that I realised. My eyes nearly popped out of my skull. 'Holy roly poly! Isn't tha—'

'You found the surprise!' exclaimed Gamble, slapping Kevin on the back. 'Nice one!'

He held the floppy thing up in the air with both hands. Even though it was completely red from the jam it was obvious what it was.

The crumper.

'You've ruined it!' I exclaimed. Immediately afterwards I realised this was a stupid thing to say: the crumper had been ruined just by being made.

Not to mention all of the awful things that had happened to it the day before.

'I'm proper clever me, innit?' said Gamble proudly. 'I cut a hole underneath the doughnut and shoved it in.'

Kevin gave a massive jammy grin. 'This is well cool! What do I win? Not the jumper, I hope. I'd rather wear someone's used verruca sock than *that*.'

I suppose he had a point there.

'Nope!' said Gamble, 'better than that. You get to give me fifty quid towards the badger charity.' Gamble turned to Vanya, 'See – told you I'd make us some money.'

'That's not a prize,' said Kevin, outraged. 'I'm not paying you a penny.'

Gamble's little forehead creased up into an angry frown. 'You'd better had do. And it *is* a prize. If you pay me the money, you get to win your teeth.'

'What do you mean?' said Kevin, narrowing his eyes suspiciously.

'Well,' shrugged Gamble, 'if you don't give me fifty quid I'll smash 'em all out.'

Gamble raised his fist and Kevin went pale like he was about to puke.

'Darren Gamble!' yelled Miss Clegg from the school doorway. Gamble froze, fist in mid-air. 'Inside now!'

''Snot fair,' moaned Gamble as he lowered his fist and traipsed inside. 'I never get to punch anyone round here.'

'And Roman and Vanya as well,' said Mrs McDonald.

Confused, Vanya and I glanced at each other before following him. I'd only gone a few steps when Rosie blocked my path. She thrust the jammed-up crumper under my chin. 'Put it on.'

'No way, Rosie,' I said. 'Look at it.'

'Well. You give me no option,' tutted Rosie. She pulled out her phone and tapped the screen. On speakerphone, I heard it ring once before it was answered.

'Hi, sweetie,' said her dad.

'Daddy, that horrible boy won't put on the jumper you sponsored him to wear.'

There was a pause. 'Well, darling . . . I'm happy to still pay the sponsorship money if it helps you to meet the princess. Anything for my little girl.'

Amazing! He was on my side.

'That works for me,' I called out to him.

'NO!' yelled Rosie into the phone, so loud it

must've burst her dad's eardrum. 'He's a nasty cheat. Tell him, Daddy, or I swear I'll cry so hard you'll have to buy me a new pony.'

'Darling. I'm in an important meeting and . . .'

'DO IT!'

On the other end of the phone Rosie's dad sighed. 'OK. Is he there? Right, young man. Well, I'll say this once. You made an agreement. And it breaks my heart to hear my little girl upset. Put on that jumper right now or pay the two hundred pounds yourself. Otherwise I'll call my lawyers. Got it?'

'What?' I exclaimed. I don't have two pounds, let alone two hundred.

'Was that OK, sweetie pie?' asked Rosie's dad.

'Thanks, Daddy dearest,' simpered Rosie, ending the call. Her face became cold as she turned to me. 'You heard him. Put that crumper on now, you revolting pig's bladder.'

I took a deep breath then pulled the sticky, smelly crumper over my head and trudged inside.

Strike One

When Vanya and I reached the classroom, Gamble was sitting opposite Mrs McDonald. Miss Clegg was next to him. She was leaning back in her chair blowing spit bubbles like this was the last place on earth she wanted to be.

'Ah, thank you for joining us,' smiled Mrs McDonald. 'And . . . er, Roman. Is that blood all over your sweater?'

Vanya and I sat down. 'It's jam, miss,' I said.

'Right. Well. Could you stop licking it please?'

I pulled the sleeve out of my mouth and forced a smile. I hadn't even noticed I'd been doing it. This was actually pretty disgusting when you consider where it'd been the night before. I had no idea if Gamble had washed it before he'd shoved it in the giant doughnut.

'Do you know why you're here?' Mrs McDonald asked.

Vanya and I shook our heads.

'I ask myself why I'm here every time I see this little rodent,' moaned Miss Clegg, jerking her head towards Gamble.

'Thank you, Miss Clegg,' said Mrs McDonald.

'Miss,' said Gamble, suddenly excited, 'is it because of your guinea pigs, miss? They're not in their cage.'

'You're right. I found a babysitter.'

'Why would you get someone to sit on a guinea

pig, miss,' said Gamble, who clearly didn't know what a babysitter was. 'I *did* once fall asleep on top of a rat but that was by accident. It'd crawled into my bed.'

Mrs McDonald screwed up her face, like someone had poured lemon juice in her eyes. 'Darren. The school had a phone call last night from a member of the public who'd seen someone matching your description doing – *ahem* – something *awful*.'

'Oh, miss, you can't be mad about that,' scoffed Gamble. 'I mean, I was desperate. And there weren't any toilets around. And how was I to know someone was gonna want to wear those wellies again? They'd just left 'em outside their front door.'

All four of us stared at him, mouths open.

'What are you all looking at?' he said. 'Everyone's done it. And it could've been worse. I could've needed a —'

'Thank you, Darren,' said Mrs McDonald, pinching her nose. 'Actually, I was referring to when you were seen biting a swan.' She turned to me and Vanya. 'Were you two there? *Did* this happen?'

I gulped and we both sort of nodded our heads.

'Thanks for grassing on me,' huffed Gamble. 'And anyway, *it* tried to bite *me* first.'

Mrs McDonald took off her glasses and let them hang round her neck on their chain. 'You do know that all swans in England belong to the royal family, don't you, Darren?'

I'd actually heard this before. Something about an old king from history wanting to hunt them all himself.

Gamble shrugged. 'So?'

'So we're meant to be meeting Princess Lucy on Friday to celebrate being kind to animals,' she said, slowly enough that he'd understand. 'Now I'm desperate for you to have the chance to meet her . . .'

'Me too,' said Gamble, 'I'm gonna cuddle her really tight and maybe I'll hide in the boot of her car so she'll drive me back to her palace and th—'

'But,' interrupted Mrs McDonald, 'there's no way I can let you if you're being cruel to animals, particularly when those animals belong to her family.'

'Amen to that,' yawned Miss Clegg. 'First sensible thing you've said in ages.'

'WHAT?!' cried Gamble, ''Snot fair! It's always been my dream to meet Princess Whojamaflip!'

This isn't quite true. It's actually always been his

dream to have a monkey butler, but I didn't think that now was the right time to point this out.

Mrs McDonald took a deep breath. 'Right. Well, we'll call that strike one. Two more and you're out, understand? And, Roman and Vanya – you two are working with him on the fundraising. Help him stay out of trouble, please.'

I opened my eyes wide. How were we supposed to do that? She might as well have asked us to teach an earthworm to juggle.

And besides that, *two more strikes?* He hadn't been banned from meeting the princess after **biting one of her swans**? I told you Mrs McDonald lets a lot of his bad behaviour go but this was incredible. What would he have to do to miss out on meeting the princess? Put her pet cat in a liquidiser?

It seemed like Miss Clegg agreed with me on this. 'Huh. I'd have had him locked up by now.'

Mrs McDonald ignored her. 'And no more cruelty to animals, Darren.'

At this moment, a wasp landed on my shoulder and began eating the jam. Terrified, I jerked my head away from it. It buzzed off, circled for a moment then landed back on the crumper again.

'Thanks, miss. I'll be kind to all living things

from now on,' said Gamble, talking to Mrs McDonald but keeping his eyes on the wasp. 'I love animals, me.'

In one fluid movement he smacked the wasp as hard as he could and flicked its lifeless body across the room.

Mrs McDonald stared at him.

'Whoops,' he grinned sheepishly.

The Most Exciting Week of All Time

When the rest of the class came in for register, Rosie collected everyone's pound coins for Wear Your Own Clothes day. Even though I'm not too bothered about fashion, I still felt rubbish being stuck in the jam-covered crumper when everyone else was wearing their own stuff. A couple more wasps circled me and I swished them away with my hand.

'I haven't brought any money,' I said to Rosie, when she came up to me.

'Doesn't surprise me,' she breezed. 'After all, you are a povtastic tramp and a vicious badger murderer.'

'No, I'm not,' I said. 'I didn't think I had to pay today. You've already sponsored me to wear the crumper.'

Rosie ignored me completely and looked expectantly at Vanya, who put two pounds in and said, 'Don't worry, I'll pay for you, Roman.'

'Yes, he is a charity case,' said Rosie, before turning back to me. 'Anyway, I thought you might like a peek at my blog.'

'Why would I?' I asked. I did actually read a bit of Rosie's fashion and beauty blog ('*How to be as Awesome as Me*') once by accident. It was full of tips like:

1) If you're too poor to afford nice clothes then you probably don't deserve to look good so don't bother.

2) Some people say that it doesn't matter what you look like. Those people are always ugly.

3) If you *are* ugly, you should wear a mask in public or just not go outside. It's not really fair to force people to look at your disgusting face.

4) However, if you're good-looking, always have at least one ugly friend. They'll make you look way more attractive when you're with them. Plus, if you're ever feeling down about yourself, you can make fun of them for being totally gross. This is a brilliant way to make yourself feel better.

It was awful.

Rosie checked herself out in her handheld mirror before snapping it shut and turning her attention back to me. 'Remember I took a snap of you yesterday? I put it out there on my blog to see what people thought of your . . . *ahem* . . . taste in clothes. And, well . . . the jury's in. See for yourself.'

She took out her phone and handed it to me with a sickly smile. There's a page on Rosie's blog called 'Groomed or Doomed', where she posts pictures of herself so that a bunch of simpletons around the world can vote on whether she looks good (groomed) or bad (doomed) and tell her how beautiful she is. The latest post was a picture of me from Monday with the title: 'My school's resident freak puts the sweat into this grimtabulous sweater – whaddya think?'

To my horror, underneath there were absolutely hundreds of comments. None of them were nice.

'What kind of a toiletbrained squirrel fart would wear something like that?' read the first one. As I scanned through the thread, everyone seemed to be trying to be nastier than the person before.

'Bad jumper. Bad face. Urgh.'

'Call the fashion police and have him put in jail for life'

The worst one, though, was from a woman called 'Fashion Nan' who looked about ninety in her profile avatar. She wrote:

'If I saw this idiot walking down the street, I'd run him over on my mobility scooter! #doingtheworldafavour'

My mouth had gone dry. OK, so the kind of people who follow Rosie's blog aren't exactly going to be the nicest people in the world, but come on – this was seriously horrible. I was being trolled by a prune-faced old woman!

'The internet can be so mean,' said Rosie, sticking out her bottom lip and doing a cry-baby voice. 'Oh. And I forgot. That jumper *stinks* of animals. ACHHHOOOO!'

She sneezed right in my face. Again.

'It hasn't been near any animals,' I said, wiping my cheeks.

'How about your mate, Gamble? He's a disgusting beast.'

At the front of the classroom, there was a fundraising chart. Miss Clegg was colouring in a few squares to show how much different people had raised so far. By the time Rosie had collected the Wear Your Own Clothes money, she was in front by an absolute mile.

'Can't wait to meet the princess,' she sang loudly, as she swished across the room in her ridiculous pirate outfit. 'I've always felt more comfortable around rich people than around penniless paupers like you lot. No offence.'

None taken.

'We *really* need to get our acts together and start raising some cash,' said Vanya, 'We can't miss out on this. It's the chance of a lifetime. And imagine if SHE won.'

I smiled weakly. I desperately wanted to help her but I didn't have any ideas.

'Well, everyone,' said Mrs McDonald, 'more news! This is shaping up to be the most exciting week of all time. We're going out of school not once but twice!'

Everyone cheered.

Miss Clegg wiped her nose on her sleeve. 'I'm not letting Darren near the general public unless he's in a cage.'

'Don't worry. I'm being good now,' said Gamble, 'so keep your hair on, hippo knickers.'

Miss Clegg ground her teeth together.

'Anyway,' continued Mrs McDonald, 'I've spoken to the wildlife hospital round the corner. We're going to have a look round tomorrow morning to see what the money from Badges for Badgers will be spent on.'

Everyone chattered excitedly.

'Letters will go out tonight. Any questions?'

Rosie cleared her throat. 'Will I be allowed to just *not* go to the wildlife hospital? I mean, ill animals are, like, *totally* depressing and I'm completely allergic, as you know. Plus I've got my fashion show tomorrow afternoon. Tickets available at five pounds each, by the way.'

She'd put huge posters for this fashion show all over school. I definitely wasn't going to go. First of all, fashion is pointless and stupid. And second, **FIVE QUID** to watch Rosie and her awful friends prance about in rubbish clothes? I couldn't think of anything worse.

'No, Rosie,' sighed Mrs McDonald. 'If you want to meet the princess on Friday then I think you should go and see what her charity is all about.'

Rosie rolled her eyes. 'Fine. Whatever. But if any

of those little critters make me sneeze, I swear I'll hide their lifesaving medicine from them then have them made into gloves.'

What a lovely girl.

A Small Flood

First lesson of the day was gymnastics on the apparatus. Luckily for me, Mrs McDonald told me to remove the crumper because she thought it could be a health and safety hazard.

Rosie wasn't happy about this at all. 'My dad's giving two hundred pounds to charity. Roman should have to wear it even if it's tied to an aeroplane that's about to take off.'

Mrs McDonald sighed. 'But what if he fell off the apparatus and it got caught on something? He could choke to death.'

'Hmm,' said Rosie, weighing this up for a moment. 'That's a risk I'm prepared to take.'

Nice to know you care.

Thankfully Mrs McDonald didn't agree with her.

The PE lesson was, as usual, pretty rubbish. We had to create a gymnastic sequence in pairs, based on the theme of being kind to animals. This seemed totally stupid to me: I mean, what were we meant to do? Save a squirrel by doing a sideways roll? Make hedgehogs healthy with a handstand? Cure a cuckoo with a cartwheel?

To make things worse, my partner was Gamble. He thought we should just 'climb to the top of the ropes then let go and see what happens'.

Luckily for me, we had to stop the lesson before he could make me do this. Kevin 'Grand Old Puke of York' Harrison had got stuck at the top of the wallbars. He was moaning that he still felt ill after the giant doughnut incident before school. His cheeks were bulging out and Mrs McDonald was trying to coax him down before there was a multicoloured rainstorm.

Unfortunately, she was too late.

I don't really want to go into detail about what happened next. Let's just say there was **An Incident**, after which the caretaker had to come along with a full bucket of sawdust, the wall bars were out of action for the rest of the day, and a couple of unfortunate children had to go to the medical room for an emergency hair wash.

Back at class, though, things got even worse.

After we'd walked into the classroom, it took us

all a few moments to realise that something was wrong. But then we noticed the buzzing sound. And the *movement* on the back of my chair.

'Sweet doughnut sandwiches!' I exclaimed.

The crumper was absolutely *alive* with wasps. There were millions of them, swarming all over it to get to the jam. It was utterly horrible, but also weirdly hypnotic. More and more wasps were buzzing through the air towards it from an open window. The crumper was like a giant wasp tractor beam.

'Try to stay calm!' said Mrs McDonald, but nobody listened to her. People edged away towards the sides of the room and one or two even ran out of the door.

'PE's over. You'd better put it back on, Roman,' said Rosie, pushing me towards the crumper.

'I'll be stung to death!' I spluttered, squirming away from her.

'Not necessarily,' she said. 'You might survive with life-changing injuries.'

I didn't like the way she seemed excited by this idea.

Amazingly, it was Gamble who saved the day. 'Coming through!' he yelled. He ran over to the crumper, grabbed it and sprinted out of the room again, holding it above his head like the Olympic torch, with a cloud of wasps buzzing around behind him.

'Where are you go—?' cried Mrs McDonald but it was too late. He'd already shoved his way through the rest of the class, who were literally scrambling over each other to get away from him. In moments, he was gone, followed by the last few straggling wasps.

Mrs McDonald looked worried. But not quite worried enough to chase him herself. 'Quick! Miss Clegg. Search the school for him.'

Miss Clegg considered this for a moment. 'Nah. I'm allergic to wasps.'

'Are you sure?' asked Mrs McDonald.

'Probably,' shrugged Miss Clegg. 'I'd better not risk it. Why don't you send Roman? He promised to look out for him.'

Mrs McDonald looked towards me hopefully. 'I *would* go myself,' she said, 'but I really should stay here and make sure everyone's OK.'

Fantastic. It didn't look like I had much say in the matter.

'Don't get too close if you find him, Roman.'

Don't worry, I thought, *I'll keep my distance.*

Although I really didn't want to go looking for Gamble, I was seriously worried that he might be hurt. He is my mate, after all, even if I've not quite figured out *why* yet.

I needed to find him fast so I ran through the school, checking all of his usual hiding places – inside the big lost property bin with all the smelly old clothes, on top of the maths cupboard, behind the photocopier – but after about five minutes of searching there was still no sign of him. Then I noticed that the caretaker's storeroom door was open. I rushed over. This is another of Gamble's favourite hide-outs: he'd once been caught in there trying to make a bomb out of cleaning products. It was empty. But a couple of the shelves seemed to have big gaps on them, and a few stray wasps buzzed around near the window. Plus there was a hint of that wet-dog-Gamble-smell in the air. I was certain he'd been here.

I was just wondering where he might have gone next when I heard some loud and imaginative swearing from inside the boys' toilets. Jackpot! Gamble is the only person I know who can swear like that. I crossed the corridor and approached the loo cautiously.

My plan was to tiptoe quietly to the door and listen through it so that if he was being stung badly by the wasps I'd be able to run away and escape.

Ahem. I mean: 'I'd be able to run away *and get help quickly.*'

But then my feet made a splashing sound on the hallway carpet. I looked down. The floor was soaked, and foamy water was streaming out from the gap under the door.

This didn't look good.

Nervously, I knocked.

'There's no one in here,' growled Gamble from inside.

I tried to push the door open but he was holding it shut. By now water was seeping in through my shoes. 'Open up, Darren. It's me. Roman.'

With a sudden gush of water, the door opened and I was dragged inside.

The whole room was a disaster zone.

The foam was waist-deep everywhere, like I was standing in a giant washing-up bowl. And underneath the foam, water was sloshing over my ankles. *But where was it coming from?* I glanced round the room and realised that there were hardly any wasps, which was at least *some* relief. A few of them were flying dizzily around the light in the ceiling, but most of them had disappeared.

'Where are they?' I asked.

Gamble had two large empty boxes under his arm, which looked like they'd once contained cleaning powder of some description. He nodded towards a closed toilet cubicle. 'Needed to wash the crumper, innit.'

It was then that I saw the source of the water and foam. It was pouring out from under the cubicle door, along with the bodies of hundreds of dead wasps. Nervously, I edged it open.

The cubicle was absolutely filled with foam, deeper than my whole body. I swept it out of the way with my arms and blew it off my face until I dug deep enough to see where it was coming from. Then I saw it. The toilet seat was down but foamy water was pouring out from under it and cascading over the rim like a waterfall. And the toilet was swooshing and gurgling like it had just been flushed. But it wasn't stopping.

'Why's it doing that?' I asked nervously.

Gamble put the boxes down then rummaged around in his pockets. I gulped as he held up the metal flush handle from the toilet. This was seriously bad.

He'd broken the bog!

One end of it was mangled where it'd obviously been wrenched off. 'It kind of came away in my hand . . .' he said, using it to scratch his head.

'But how?'

He looked suddenly cross at me. 'It's all your stupid fault, innit? I had to flush proper hard to get enough water.'

'What are you talking about?'

When Gamble didn't answer, a horrible, hollow feeling built up in my guts. I carefully lifted the toilet seat, scooped the foam off the top of the pouring water and peered into the loo. And then I saw it. Amongst the last few dead wasps, an unmistakable brown woolly arm was sticking out from the U-bend, waving like seaweed in the high toilet water. I was gripped with cold fear. 'You *flushed* my crumper down the loo? Are you insane?'

Gamble huffed. 'I had to. I needed somewhere to wash it. It was the only way to kill the wasps.'

This was ridiculous. Only Darren Gamble could wash my jumper in a toilet then blame *me* when it all went wrong. The water continued to rush out uncontrollably. I stepped back, realising it was splashing down my school trousers. 'Why didn't you use the sink?'

Gamble looked confused. 'What?'

I pointed over to it. 'The sink! You know, the bowl you wash your hands in.'

'Is *that* what it's for?' he asked, eyes open wide. 'Oh! I thought it was a mini toilet for doing wees in.'

I did my best to ignore this. Of course – when had Gamble ever washed his hands? 'What are we going to do now?'

Gamble sniffed. 'Well, I was thinking of shoving one of the Year Ones down there to push it through. Their heads should be small enough to fit down the pipe, I reckon.'

I pinched the top of my nose. 'So you plan to unblock the toilet by using a six-year-old as a human bog brush?'

'Pretty much, yeah.'

'Definitely not. We've got to pull it out. Otherwise we'll be in mega-trouble.'

'Well, I'm not putting my hand down a toilet. It's unhygienic.'

If the situation hadn't been so serious, this

would've made me laugh. Hygiene isn't usually Gamble's main priority. You could grow potatoes under his fingernails and he's always doing gross stuff. One lunchtime ('for a laugh') he put a handful of his dog's bum worms in someone's stir-fried noodles.

There was a knock on the door. Quick as a flash, Gamble skated over and slammed himself up against it.

The person on the other side pounded on the frosted glass panel. 'Let me in. It's an emergency.'

Oh great. It was Kevin Harrison. That's all we needed.

I thought Gamble might take pity on him but he didn't budge. 'Toilet's engaged so get lost, Ali Blargh-blargh and the Forty Heaves.'

Even though this wasn't exactly the best time to appreciate it, I have to say I quite liked this new nickname for Kevin. Under other circumstances I might even have applauded it, but the water was getting deeper by the second and there was no time to lose.

'But . . .' said Kevin from the other side of the door.

'Why don't you go chuck up in your lunchbox?'

suggested Gamble helpfully. We heard Kevin stagger away towards the cloakroom.

'Right,' said Gamble, suddenly businesslike. 'We don't have long. It's your jumper so you'd better deal with it.'

'That's not fair,' I said. 'And what am I supposed to do with a soaking wet toilet crumper?'

'Shove it under the dryer and put it back on. It'll be as good as new.'

'It'll stink!' I exclaimed.

'They'll be suspicious if you're not wearing it.'

'And what about the massive flood?' I said.

Gamble twitched. 'Pretend we didn't see nothing. Not our problem'.

Of course, I knew that this was a terrible idea. But what else could I do? I rolled up my sleeve. And then, holding my nose and trying not to think about what had been down there in the past, I plunged my hand into that cold, disgusting water and grabbed hold of the crumper. With one huge yank, I pulled it clear.

And it was at that exact moment the door flew open.

'Roman!' cried Mrs McDonald. 'What on earth are you doing?'

Rosie was at her shoulder. 'You'd better put that crumper back on *now*.'

Strike Two

Needless to say, Gamble got given his second strike. He tried to plead that he was only trying to get rid of the wasps, but Mrs McDonald thought that was no excuse for turning the toilet into a foam party. In a massive huff, Gamble ran outside and climbed onto the roof of the PE shed. Miss Clegg was delighted about this: she had to go out there with him to 'make sure he didn't hurt himself'. She spent the whole afternoon sunbathing on the field.

Meanwhile, Rosie refused to let me get away with not wearing the toilet crumper.

'It's for those poor sick badgers,' she said, a mocking smile across her lips.

In the end I had to wear it again. I'd put it under the hand dryer but it was still damp, and along with the dead maggots, there were also a fair few dead wasps in amongst the stitching, which I had to carefully pluck out so they didn't sting me. It didn't take long for people to notice the smell either.

'It's gross!' someone howled. 'Smells like a penguin's armpit.'

'More like a skunk's boobs,' moaned someone else.

'It *is* a bit ripe,' Mrs McDonald, throwing open the windows. A couple of people rushed over and stuck their heads out for fresh air.

My face hot and flushed, I turned to my left. Vanya tried to smile. 'It's not as awful as you think, Roman,' she whispered. I might have believed her if her eyes weren't watering at the time.

Eventually, the whole class (including Vanya) spread out away from me in a wide circle, holding their noses.

'He can't help himself,' said Rosie, pursing her lips. 'He's not been potty-trained for very long.'

'It's not me. It's the jumper,' I protested.

'You'll have to take it off,' said Mrs McDonald. 'Rosie – could you ask the caretaker for one of those hazardous waste bags?'

'I'm not going anywhere,' snapped Rosie, 'and Roman is *not* changing out of that crumper. He's been sponsored, remember?'

Everyone else groaned.

'Now come on, Rosie,' said Mrs McDonald, 'for the good of the class . . .'

But Rosie shook her head. 'And what would we say to Princess Lucy on Friday? *Sorry, Your Royal Highness. We tried to raise two hundred quid for the badgers but Roman stinks like a baboon's nappy so I'm afraid they're all going to have to die in pain.* Hashtag: keep it on.'

'Well . . . er . . .' began Mrs McDonald.

'So,' continued Rosie, smiling at me with one side of her mouth, 'he'll just have to sit outside in his own filth like the disgusting brute he is.'

And that was that. I had to take my book out and sit next to Miss Clegg on the field. Rosie followed me at a safe distance so she could warn Miss Clegg 'not to even think about letting me take it off'.

To make me smell better, Miss Clegg squirted me with her perfume, which was called *Irresistible Woman*. Amazingly it smelled even worse than the toilet crumper – like an overpowering cocktail of burning car tyres and rotting vegetables. After getting a whiff of it, Rosie snatched it off her, removed the lid and poured half the bottle all over me. 'That should do it!'

'Thanks,' I said flatly. Where she'd poured it, a patch of the woolly crumper was slowly losing its colour and turning white. Underneath, I felt a faint tingling on my skin. What was in that stuff? Acid?

I didn't know which was worse — smelling like a toilet or smelling like Miss Clegg on a date. Either way, it didn't really matter. The crumper had made my life more complicated than ever before. But things were only going to get worse.

Life doesn't get any better than that

As I was coming out through the school gates that afternoon, Rosie Taylor was trying to flog her fashion show tickets for Wednesday. When I walked past, she dramatically pulled them away from me. 'You can't have one, Roman. Hashtag: no freaks allowed.'

'I don't really want one,' I replied.

'Course you do. Everyone does.'

I didn't agree with her here. As far as I could tell, she hadn't sold a single ticket yet. Rosie didn't seem worried, though. 'I've even invited Princess Lucy.'

'Do you think she'll come?'

Rosie pursed her lips. 'Er . . . *of course* she will. She *loves* fashion and she *loves* badgers too so she'll definitely be here and she'll be like: *Ooh, Rosie. You're sooooo supercool. Let's be BFFs and then we can gang up on Roman and have him executed for crimes against fashion.*'

The worst thing was, I think that she genuinely believed this was going to happen. I shook my head. 'Good luck with that.'

I walked home just with Vanya. Gamble said I stank too bad to walk with, which was a bit rich coming from a kid who once went a whole month without changing his socks. Vanya and I didn't talk much on the way home. This was mainly because she wanted to stay far enough away from me so that she couldn't smell me. But we were also deep in thought about different things. She was trying to come up with more fundraising ideas, while I was more worried about how upset Grandma would be when she saw the state of the crumper. I'd tried to dab it clean at school but I couldn't get rid of all the jam or dead wasps, and the white patch now covered most of one shoulder.

By the time we went off in different directions, Vanya still hadn't thought of an idea, and I felt like I was carrying a massive cannonball of guilt round in my belly.

I was right to be concerned.

When Grandma saw the crumper, she inspected it closely, using her thick specs like a magnifying glass. 'Patches of red stuff . . . dead *beasties* . . . you've bleached it here . . . and pooeee! It smells like a dead squid . . .' She peered up into my eyes. 'Haven't you been looking after it? Don't you . . . *like* it?'

'I . . . er . . .' I spluttered. Her face was so *hurt* – she looked like Mrs McDonald did that time when Gamble gave her some anti-wrinkle cream and weight loss tablets for Christmas.

'Course he does!' said Mum quickly.

'Yes, of course I do,' I agreed, suddenly coming up with an idea. 'In fact, I'd like to wear it every day this week.'

Grandma's face cracked into a brilliant smile. 'Really?'

'Yes,' I said, which was technically not a lie. Admittedly, I only wanted to wear it so that I didn't get in trouble with Rosie's dad. But still, Grandma didn't need to know that.

'Great,' said Mum. 'Let's shove it in the washing machine so it's nice and clean for tomorrow. Might as well wash your trousers as well.'

I hate it when Mum makes me strip off my

uniform at the door. Imagine if someone suddenly came round when I was standing in the hallway in my pants. They'd think I was a weirdo. Quick as I could, I dumped my trousers on the floor and ran upstairs to have a shower.

I had one foot over the rim of the bath when Mum called up to me. 'What are these letters in your pocket about, Roman? One's from yesterday. You didn't tell us your class was going to see Princess Lucy on Friday. And a trip to a wildlife hospital as well?'

I hadn't meant to keep the letters from her. I guess that, with all the troubles I'd been having over the last few days, I'd just forgotten to hand them over. I wrapped myself in a towel and came to the top of the stairs. 'Oh yeah. Sorry about that. I think you need to sign the forms.'

But it wasn't Mum who answered. Grandma had snatched one of the letters off her and was now squinting at it from a couple of millimetres away. 'Oh *my* . . . three people to meet Princess Lucy . . . everyone else to be there when she arrives . . .' She staggered back a couple of steps and leaned against the bottom of the bannister.

'Everything OK, Grandma?' I said uneasily.

Grandma wiped a little tear from her eye. 'Oh, this is wonderful! Wonderful! Imagine, **my** grandson wearing **my** jumper in front of **my** favourite member of the royal family. Life doesn't get any better than that! The newspapers will be there. And the television cameras. People all over the world would see you and the princess and my jumper. How marvellous!'

'Yes,' I croaked. 'Marvellous.'

WEDNESDAY

Morning

When the Crumper Changed Size and Gamble Entertained Some Wildlife

'Well, I still think it looks lovely,' said Mum, looking and sounding like she didn't really believe what she was saying. 'Despite the fact it's . . . *changed* a bit.'

'We're going to the wildlife hospital this morning,' I whined. 'Even the injured squirrels will bully me.'

Mum pursed her lips. 'That's probably not going to happen.'

Probably. I rolled my eyes. This was a disaster. The crumper had been bad enough before but now it had plunged to new depths. The night before, once Grandma had learned about the royal visit, she'd insisted on taking charge of washing it herself.

I think I've already mentioned about Grandma's poor eyesight. Well, she'd accidentally put the crumper in the washing machine on a super-hot temperature. The body had shrunk to about a third of its previous size so now it didn't even stretch over my chubby doughnut belly. On the front of it, Princess Lucy's face had also shrivelled, like a picture. Unfortunately, this just made the cone-shaped eye-boobs stick out even further.

But, worst of all, the arms had stayed the same length because they were made of a different wool which didn't shrink in the wash. I looked completely stupid. Imagine a heavily pregnant woman in a crop top crossed with Mr Tickle and you get the idea.

Just then Grandma came into the room. Mum and I stopped talking about the crumper straight away.

'Oooh! Don't you look handsome?' cooed Grandma. I told you her eyesight was bad. She waggled my cheek so hard that she let out one of those trumps old ladies do whenever they move too vigorously.

I held my breath and tried to smile.

I didn't have a choice about wearing it, of course. That morning a letter had been delivered to the house. It was from Rosie's dad and said that 'his daughter's happiness was the most important thing in the world' so he just wanted to repeat 'how serious it was that the jumper was worn **at all times**' or 'there will be consequences'. I could just imagine Rosie standing over him while he typed it.

As soon as I'd read the letter I'd torn it up and thrown it in the bin so that Grandma didn't see it. I didn't want her to know I was only wearing the crumper because I was being forced to.

Broken Badger

Of course, Rosie noticed the shrinkage as soon as I walked into class an hour later.

'WOW! Nice boob tube, Roman!' she exclaimed. 'Has the crumper shrunk or are you comfort eating because you're depressed at how horrible your clothes are? You look like that American pop star Todd Gelatine. He had a breakdown and ate forty cheeseburgers a day. Hashtag: here comes fatty-fatty boom-boom.'

Blushing, I tried to stretch the front of the crumper down so it at least got close to my belly button.

'Settle down, everyone,' said Mrs McDonald, who was standing in front of the fundraising chart. 'Before the register, I suppose you'd like to know who's raised the most money for the badgers so far.'

'Definitely,' said Rosie smugly.

'Well ta-*da*!' said Mrs McDonald, stepping to the side.

Even from near the back of the room, it was clear that Rosie was winning by miles. Her coloured bar showed that she'd raised over four hundred pounds in just a couple of days. In fact, Mrs McDonald had had to extend the chart by a whole extra piece of A3 to fit it all on. The next best was Kevin '*Ali Blargh Blargh and the Forty Heaves*' Harrison, who'd raised six pounds by doing a sponsored 'Drink as Much Milkshake as You Can in a Minute'. I hated to think what had happened next but I figured he might've raised even more if he'd also done a sponsored Puke Your Guts Up as well. After him came my ex-girlfriend, Jane Dixon, who'd done a Readathon. Everyone else in the class was somewhere behind her. Vanya, Gamble and I were in last place with 10p between us from the giant doughnut sale.

'We'll sort it out,' whispered Vanya, squeezing my arm. I wasn't quite sure how this was going to happen though. Not with Gamble in our group anyway. And in any case, did I *really* want to meet the princess wearing the crumper? There'd be TV cameras there and everything. Maybe it would be better for everyone if I just stepped aside and let Vanya meet her. It seemed like it meant a lot more to her than it did to me.

'I've been thinking,' I said. 'I'm not sure I want to meet the princess after all. You can keep my share of the money.'

Vanya's eyes opened wide in surprise. 'Don't be silly, Roman. You'll never get a chance like this again. You've got to go for it. And anyway, I don't want to meet Princess Lucy standing next to Rosie, do I?'

I shrugged. Maybe she was right. But then again, it wasn't her who'd have to wear the crumper in front of the whole world.

Gamble turned round to face us. Although he had big black rings round his eyes, he was grinning excitedly and bouncing around. This was not a good sign. I'll explain why later.

'I've got an idea,' he said. 'How about we do some busking in town?'

'Not heavy metal music,' sighed Vanya. 'I don't

think people will pay money to listen to you wail some deafening song like "Ostrich Nose Wipe" by the Chainsaw Lickers.'

Gamble ground his teeth together. 'Actually, everyone loves the Chainsaw Lickers. Even my great-granddad. And anyway, I was thinking more about the armpit orchestra.' He shoved his hand into his sweaty pit and jerked his arm up and down to make a squelchy farting noise.

'Why did I let you put me in a group with him?' asked Vanya. I tried to force a smile. Clearly, we weren't going to get anywhere with the fundraising any time soon.

'Can't wait to meet the princess,' simpered Rosie loudly to no one in particular. Whenever there's a moment of silence, she likes to fill it by talking about herself. 'This is my big chance.'

'Big chance of what?' I said, turning round.

Rosie tutted. 'Of being accepted into the royal inner circle.'

'What *are* you talking about?'

'OMG, Roman,' she snorted, 'I know you've got a face like a goat's nipple but I'd no idea you had a brain like one as well.'

I was too busy trying to picture what a goat's

nipple looks like to answer her. Rosie ran her fingers through her hair and continued.

'So, this afternoon, I'm going to meet Princess Lucy at my fashion show and she's going to be like, *wow. Who is* THAT?! *She's so well dressed and beautiful that I wish she'd be my friend.*'

'I don't think that will happ—' I began, but Rosie carried on talking, becoming more and more excited with every word.

'. . . then we'll Snapchat each other a few times and I'll be like *"see you on Friday at Daddy's shopping centre"*, then after that we'll hang out together and become besties and go on girly shopping trips and family ski holidays and I'll be like her fashion adviser and I'll tell her what to wear and one day she might even let me move into the palace and then I'll be a princess too and I'll spend the rest of my life teaching royalty and celebs how to be beautiful like me.'

Her face was flushed and her eyes were bulging and goggly. It reminded me of the time Gamble told me how he'd found a dead frog and inflated it with a straw up its bum 'until its head burst'.

'Are you completely demented?' I asked her.

Suddenly angry, Rosie jutted out her lower jaw.

'You have no idea what this means to me. This is literally my only chance to become a real-life princess. And I'm not going to stop until I do.'

'That's the spirit, Rosie!' said Mrs McDonald. 'Keep on raising money for the badgers.'

'The *what*?' said Rosie.

'The badgers.'

Rosie looked like she'd just stepped barefoot on a slug. 'Oh yeah. Of course. It's all about the badgers.'

Where's These Badgers At?

After the register we set off straight away. Our school is quite near the edge of town so if you walk for five minutes in the right direction you're almost in the countryside. On the way, Vanya and I tried to talk about new fundraising ideas but we drew a complete blank. It was getting more and more unlikely all the time that we'd raise enough.

On the one hand, this made me feel quite relieved. If we didn't come in the top three then I wouldn't have to stand in front of a massive crowd, a load of cameras and the world's most stylish woman while wearing the worst jumper of all time.

But then this relief caused me to feel really guilty. I didn't want to let Vanya or Grandma down. And I really *did* want to help the badgers. After a while I fell into miserable silence. The whole thing was giving me serious brain-ache.

After a short while, we turned off the main road and followed the pavement along a quiet lane. Slowly the houses became more and more spaced out until we reached a bungalow with a huge front garden and large wooden gates by the side of it. The sign outside read:

'BROKEN BADGER ANIMAL WELFARE CENTRE WE MEND MOLES, FIX FOXES, REPAIR RABBITS AND MORE!'

As we crunched along the gravel driveway, Rosie sniffed the air then pulled a white face mask up over her mouth. 'This is going to be disgusting.'

Gamble was wearing a set of reins, like the ones that toddlers have, and Miss Clegg was holding the other end in her huge doughy fist. 'Oh, I can't wait for this,' he panted, straining at the leash like an excited spaniel. 'Do you reckon there'll be any blood and guts on the floor?'

Miss Clegg yanked him back. 'Yours if you don't behave.'

I wasn't surprised by Gamble's behaviour, by the way. He always stays up late on a Tuesday night to watch his favourite TV shows on the Crime and Punishment Channel (a double-bill of *America's Grisliest Murders*, followed by *When Circus Freaks Attack*). As a result, he usually struggles to keep himself awake on a Wednesday without a bit of extra help. The whole way here, he'd been glugging from a two-litre bottle of his favourite energy drink – *Wild Panic* – which he was carrying under his coat. He used to prefer one called *Electric Hyper* but then he found out about this stuff. *Wild Panic* is four times as strong, and was originally developed in North Korea to stop horses from falling asleep when they were working in underground coal mines.

Miss Clegg had ignored him drinking it, which I think was a massive mistake. By the time we reached the animal hospital, the *Wild Panic* had properly kicked in. He was foaming at the sides of his mouth and his eyes were pretty much popping out of his skull. I shuffled as far away from him as I could.

A jolly lady came out of the bungalow to greet us. Earlier I said that people's clothes tell you a lot about them. This lady was wearing wellies, scruffy trousers and a mucky green fleece with an 'I heart badgers' T-shirt underneath. She even had hair a bit like a badger's – black and frizzy with a grey stripe along her centre parting. I don't want to be cruel but she looked as though she probably smelled like a rabbit hutch.

'Welcome,' she smiled, 'I'm Sue. We'll head round in a moment to see the animals that we look after. I know you're meeting Princess Lucy on Friday so you'll be excited to see our badgers . . .'

'Frankly I'd rather stick broken glass into my eyeballs,' huffed Rosie from behind her mask.

Sue didn't seem to hear her. 'Any questions?' she said, her huge smile spread across her face.

'Will you be going to see the princess on Friday?' Rosie asked.

Sue nodded. 'Oh yes. Our wildlife hospital will benefit from money raised by Badges for Badgers so it's very important we show our support.'

Rosie looked her up and down. 'And are you planning on wearing *that* outfit?'

'Well. Er . . .'

'Cos no offence, but the princess is really stylish, and you don't want to turn up looking like you've just been dragged through a farmer's wardrobe.'

'Rosie!' said Mrs McDonald.

'*Sorry,*' said Rosie, rolling her eyes. 'Hashtag: just trying to help. The princess is coming to my fashion show this afternoon. I'd better warn her there might be some . . . er . . . clothing disasters on display on Friday.'

I decided not to mention to her how unlikely it was that the princess was going to turn up to her fashion show.

Her smile fading slightly, Sue looked around for any other questions. Gamble's hand shot up and she pointed to him.

'You'll regret that,' yawned Miss Clegg.

Gamble's little head twitched. 'Do you ever get the animals to fight each other?'

Sue's smile had now completely disappeared. 'Excuse me?'

Before anyone else could speak, Gamble blurted out. 'Who'd win in a fight between a giant nuclear rat and a fox with a machine gun?'

Sue seemed confused. I don't blame her: not many

people have met anyone like Gamble before. 'Well.
I . . .'

'Have you ever seen a deer with two bums? Who
does the smelliest poo – dolphins or seals? What
would happen if you put a man's brain inside a
snail?'

Looking slightly disturbed, Sue backed away
from him.

'Sorry about him – he gets a little . . . excitable,'
said Mrs McDonald to Sue, before leaning into
Gamble. 'One more strike. Remember?'

Miss Clegg dragged him back towards her by his
reins.

'Shall we just . . . go round, perhaps?' said Sue.

Through a gate, the path led to an enormous
field, which had been split into smaller paddocks.
Most of them had animals in them – fat, ancient-
looking hares, a limping deer with patchy fur, a pair
of fox cubs that were fighting over a piece of rope.
Here and there, people dressed like Sue wandered
around with buckets of food, tossing scoops of it
into the enclosures. There were two buildings a bit
like the mobile classrooms at school – Sue said one
was for treating the animals, the other was a heated
room for escaped snakes and lizards.

Gamble asked her if he could milk the venom out of the poisonous snakes to use on his enemies but Sue pretended not to hear him.

'This place is rubbish. You can't do anything,' moaned Gamble. He took a massive glug of *Wild Panic* and shivered.

This wasn't going to end well.

Sue waved her arm to demonstrate the space behind her. 'As you can see, all kinds of animals are brought to us here. Some have been hit by cars or trapped in fences, others have lost their mums or been abandoned by their owners. The other night we even got a call about a swan that someone had *bitten*, would you believe?'

Gamble nearly choked on his energy drink. Mrs McDonald shifted uncomfortably.

'Luckily we found her. She was OK and we didn't need to bring her in,' Sue continued.

Phew! At least Gamble hadn't caused any lasting damage.

He seemed a bit agitated about the swan though and he raised his hand again. Sue didn't seem to want to speak to him but he asked the question anyway. 'Is it true the royal family own all the swans in the country?'

Sue seemed pleased with this rather more normal question. 'That's right, yes.'

'So if one was injured, Princess Lucy might get cross or sad?' he asked, suddenly sounding upset. His bottom lip was wobbling a little.

Sue tilted her head to one side and gave him a sweet smile. 'Probably. She *is* an animal lover.'

'So she'd need cheering up then?' sniffed Gamble.

I raised my eyebrow at him. 'What are you planning?'

Gamble took another glug of his energy drink. 'Nuffink. Where's these badgers at then?'

A Wild Party

The artificial badger sett was right at the back of the field. It was inside a large paddock, enclosed by a high mesh fence. At the far end was a grassy mound about two metres high and five metres long. The mound had all these wide tunnels dug into it, which were made of plastic tubing. In front of each one, there was a pile of trodden-down, sandy earth where the badgers came in and out.

Sue unlocked the gate of the enclosure and we all filed in. 'Now, do please be quiet. Badgers are shy creatures.'

'Can we crawl into the tunnels and make friends with them?' asked Gamble, swallowing more *Wild Panic*.

'No,' said Sue. 'We'll stay out here because we don't want to disturb them.'

'This sounds dangerous,' said Rosie. 'Shall we just give it a miss and, like, go back to school so I can set up my fashion show?'

'Well, yes, badgers *are* very strong and they *do* have sharp teeth and claws,' replied Sue, 'however they're asleep at the moment, deep under the mound, so we're perfectly safe. They only come out at night. Here . . .'

She pulled out a long rubber hose with a funnel on the end then poked it down into one of the dark tunnels. 'Perhaps this young lady would like to go first,' she said.

Nobody stepped forward. It was then that I realised she was talking to me. 'I'm a boy,' I said flatly. I look nothing like a girl. Well, apart from . . .

'Oh sorry,' said Sue, blushing, 'It's because of the . . .'

Her eyes flicked towards my chest for a millisecond and she caught the word in her throat. A few people sniggered.

Huffing out my cheeks, I flattened the crumper-boobs and stepped forward. Then I put my ear to the funnel and listened. I have to say that, even though I had to block out everyone else's laughter, it was brilliant! I could actually hear the badgers snoring from underground. For two seconds I almost forgot I was dressed like a total wally.

After we'd all had a turn, Sue led us to a large shed at the edge of the paddock. Ten people, including Gamble, went in first while the rest of us waited outside. A few minutes later, nine of them came out looking excited and saying things like: *So sweet! Amazing! That was ace!*

Gamble slouched out last. 'BORING!' he announced, head twitching something chronic. 'As if you sleep during the day?'

'Wish I could sleep during the day,' Miss Clegg muttered.

I went into the shed with Mrs McDonald and the next group.

Inside there were three monitors on the wall, which showed grainy black-and-white CCTV footage of inside the sett. You could see the badgers all snuggling up to each other in their beds of dried grass. Occasionally one would shuffle about a bit before resettling. I have to say it was pretty cool. I hadn't expected anything so hi-tech but Sue said it was important they could monitor them. 'This is why we need money from charities like Badges for Badgers,' she said. 'It's an expensive business looking after sick animals.'

The badgers were so cute, all snuggled up underground. I looked over at Vanya and smiled. It made me feel like we *definitely* had to come up with some way of raising some serious cash for them, whether we ended up meeting the princess or not.

'So we've currently got six badgers living in the sett,' said Sue. 'The most recent arrival, Hoppalong, was brought in last week with very bad injuries to his back legs. We're trying to see if he'll ever recover and . . . oh no! Is the roof leaking again?'

We all squinted at the screen. Sue was right; something seemed to be dripping down onto the badgers. At first it didn't seem to bother them but then they started wriggling about. One of them woke up, crawled over and licked the floor next to the opening of a tunnel. It shivered then lapped at it again. In doing so, it stood on a second badger, which woke up and did the same.

'Bit odd,' remarked Sue, zooming in with the camera using a small remote control, 'they should be sleeping at this time. And what *is* that liquid? It's not raining, is it?'

Within a minute, all of the badgers were wide awake, their eyes glowing brightly in the night-vision camera. They were squabbling and wrestling, butting heads and crawling over each other in a bid to drink up the dripping liquid. I'm not a badger expert but this seemed like pretty aggressive behaviour to me.

'What's going on?' cried Sue. 'This is not normal!'

It must've been the words 'not normal' that made me instinctively look out through the door for Gamble. When I saw him, my eyes opened wide with horror.

He was holding the funnel and pouring his whole bottle of *Wild Panic* down it and into one of the badger holes. When he ran out of drink, he pulled out his mobile phone and played loud, thumping heavy metal music down the tube as well. 'Badger rave, innit!' he screamed into the funnel. 'Wake up, you lazy, stripy idiots!'

I looked back at the screen. The badgers were madly licking the last few drips of energy drink. One of them was thrashing about, nutting the camera. Another one seemed to be dancing or having a fit. The rest were bustling about and charging at each other. And then . . .

'Quick! We've got to get out!' cried Sue. 'They're coming up!'

There was a mad scramble to get out of the shed, and by the time I got outside, all six of the badgers were loose, zipping around the paddock on their stumpy legs and snapping their jaws at my scattering classmates. Everyone else made it through the gate but, just as I was crossing the enclosure, the badgers cut me off. I was surrounded. And let me tell you, there is nothing more terrifying than being at the centre of a ring of angry badgers high on energy drinks and heavy metal music.

I'd never been this close to a badger before. They were like really powerful squat dogs, about knee-high to me. Bristling with anger and excitement, they flicked their stripy heads around and bared their enormous sharp teeth.

'Get out of there!' cried Sue.

'No, stay in there for a while,' said Rosie Taylor, rubbing her hands together. 'They seem hungry.'

Panicking, I glanced desperately around me. The badgers were slowly closing in. One of them – it must've been Hoppalong – seemed to be dragging its back legs, like it was badly injured.

There was only one thing for it. I screamed like a two-year-old and hurdled the limping badger. But as I jumped, one of the others leapt up and grabbed the long, dangling sleeve of my crumper. I landed but it didn't let go. It had me. The badger clamped the sleeve in between its strong jaws, tearing its head from side to side. I tried to pull away but suddenly another one had the other sleeve. I was in serious danger of being dragged to the ground and savaged.

I felt arms grabbing me round my waist and shoulders. Sue and Vanya were having a tug of war with the badgers and I was the rope!

The sleeves stretched to almost twice their original length then there was a loud ripping sound. All three of us fell backwards in a heap. The sleeves had been torn off. We leapt to our feet, scrabbling through the gate and slamming it behind us. By now, four of the badgers were fighting over the crumper sleeves. Another one flung itself at the fence, teeth bared against the mesh in a mad frenzy. Then they pulled the sleeves back towards the hole and disappeared. All except for Hoppalong, that is, who sort of flopped down on the grass and lay there panting.

'Probably shouldn't have given them the *Wild Panic*,' sniffed Gamble, in the understatement of the year. 'Still – at least we know they like it now.'

I looked at him in total disbelief.

'Who was meant to be looking after this boy?' demanded Sue.

At that moment, Miss Clegg waddled along the path. 'Sorry about that. I was desperate for the loo. Did I miss something?'

Third Strike

So the crumper had caused me to be attacked by wild animals. It now looked less like a sweater and more like a bikini top.

Of course, we were immediately asked to leave the wildlife hospital and told never to return. When we got back to school, Gamble was given his third strike, which meant he was banned from going to see the princess on Friday. Vanya also officially kicked him out of our fundraising group. For the rest of the morning he lay curled up inside the art cupboard, howling like a wounded dog.

Despite everything, I have to say I felt a bit sorry for him. I mean, he'd only been trying to cheer the badgers up. It wasn't Gamble's fault that he was entirely useless at everything.

Not having him around did kind of make it easier for Vanya and I to think of fundraising ideas, though. Vanya suggested doing a sponsored run on Thursday. I told her I would help by cheering her on. I'm about as good at running as a jellyfish in high heels.

At the time, it seemed like this would be the best I could do. But things were about to change.

At the end of lunchtime, we all came back inside to find Rosie storming around the classroom in hysterics. Mrs McDonald was trying to calm her down. On the far side of the room a group of girls were sitting with arms folded, looking cross.

'Calm down?' shrieked Rosie. 'How can I calm down? My fashion show starts in five minutes. Princess Lucy hasn't bothered to turn up. My stylist Antonio is stuck in traffic. I haven't sold a single ticket. And now my models have quit on me. This is all *Roman*'s fault.'

'Eh?' I said. 'What did I do?'

Rosie looked at me disgustedly. 'That . . . *jumper*. It destroyed fashion forever. No wonder the world's out to get me.'

'Well, I *was* a bit unhappy that you wanted to run your fashion show during class time,' said Mrs McDonald as carefully as possible, 'and I *did* say that five pounds was a lot of money for a ticket.'

Rosie's eyes opened wide like dinner plates. 'What are you talking about? Five pounds is nothing. I'm teaching people how to look good. And judging by the mingalicious threads on show at Wear Your Own Clothes Day yesterday, I think that everyone in here needs to learn *that* lesson way more than anything *you* could ever teach them.'

Mrs McDonald cleared her throat. 'And that brings me to my next point. No wonder your models quit when you speak to people like that.'

'O to the M to the G,' snapped Rosie. 'All I did was ask them if they could pleeeeaaaaassssse stop looking quite so fat and ugly. Is that too much to ask? They could've ripped my expensive clothes.'

'There's nothing else for it,' said Mrs McDonald. 'You'll have to cancel.'

'Not a chance!' roared Rosie, and she got straight on her phone. 'Daddy. It's me. I'm sad. You need to pay for my whole class to come to my fashion show otherwise I'll be cross and I'll never forgive you and when you're old I'll put you in a home and I'll pop the tyres on your wheelchair.'

Wow.

She hung up. 'Sorted. Daddy's paying. You're all coming.'

I groaned. This was going to be seriously lame. 'How can you have a fashion show without models?'

'Easy,' she said. '*I'll* model everything. I'm way better looking than anyone else anyway.'

Mrs McDonald tutted. 'No no no. Why don't you get other people to help? Roman. You've got a nice taste in clothes.'

She obviously didn't mean this and she'd only said it because I was closest to her. I mean, had she *seen* the crumper?

I was about to say I'd rather not when Rosie cried out: '*That* grotesque little goblin? You are *kidding* me!'

'It's for the badgers. And you're not having the

fashion show unless you allow others to model for you,' Mrs McDonald said calmly, before turning to me. 'Maybe Rosie could donate some of the takings to your fundraising group, Roman?'

'Yes! Go for it!' said Vanya, nodding.

'*Fine!* Ruin my life,' huffed Rosie. 'He can have, *like*, three quid.'

Gamble crawled out of the cupboard, suddenly excitable again. 'Pickmepickmepickmepickme!'

'OK, Darren,' chuckled Mrs McDonald. 'Nice to see you've cheered up.'

See? She never holds his bad behaviour against him.

Hand against her temple, Rosie stormed off towards the hall. 'Hashtag: let's get it over with.'

Natural Beauty

'I'm not doing it!' I said to Rosie. It was fifteen minutes later. We were standing in the PE cupboard at the back of the hall. The curtain was closed and, outside, the class was waiting for the show to start.

She rolled her eyes. 'Do you think *I* want you out there making me look bad? Just wear what you've been told to and shut your miserable gob.'

'I don't understand why I couldn't just take off the crumper and wear something normal,' I said, pointing my eyes down at my costume.

'Because you've been *sponsored*, you gormless chicken brain,' she sighed. 'And there's no way you're wearing any of *my* clothes. Look at the shape of you! You've got a body like a dropped trifle.'

'Thanks a lot,' I said. Not that I would've wanted to wear her clothes in the first place. 'But why do I have to dress like *this*?'

'The fashion show is called *Natural Beauty*,' she said, pouting. 'A bit like me.'

I'm not sure that *natural* beauty is the term I'd use to describe Rosie, or the way she was dressed. Her face was painted silver and she was wearing a matching catsuit with fish scales printed on it. Balanced on her head was the most ridiculous giant top hat I've ever seen: it was about two feet tall and made of hard see-through plastic. Inside, it was filled with water. There were even real live fish swimming around inside it.

She'd said that this was a 'daring outfit that was making a statement'. The only statement it seemed to be making to me was: 'Rosie Taylor is a complete nutcase.' She looked like the world's worst aquarium thief.

I, on the other hand, was dressed like a tree.

Yes, a *tree*.

My costume was a long cardboard tube with a tiny hole cut out for my face. My arms were stuck out to the side like branches, and leaves sprouted out of my head. I could hardly move, apart from a tiny shuffle of my feet.

At that moment, Gamble showed up. He was dressed as a fox. Rosie had said our costumes were originally for the 'most grim-looking models', and that 'only the decent ones got to wear the proper clothes'.

'Ready,' he said, before pretending to bark like a dog.

'You've cheered up,' I said. 'Thought you were upset about missing the princess on Friday?'

He grinned to himself. 'I came up with a plan when I was in the cupboard. You'll see.'

I didn't like the sound of that at all but I didn't have time to worry about it. From the other side of the curtain, we could see the lights in the hall go off. Some dance music started playing and Rosie shoved me out and up onto the catwalk.

Rosie had set up the stage so it went in a long strip across the middle of the hall like a runway, with the class sitting on the floor either side. I was meant to walk along it then turn around at the end and come back. This was virtually impossible though, as I could barely move my feet in the cardboard tube.

'This is Roman,' said Rosie, through a mic. 'He's dressed as a tree because he's just like one: massive, thick and home to millions of insects.'

A few people tittered.

This was *awful*. I decided to speed up to get it over with. Unfortunately that was when things started to go even worse. I could barely move in the ridiculous costume and I was already almost falling over when Gamble came bounding out onto the stage in his fox's outfit. He ran up to me, sniffed my ankles, then pretended to cock his leg and do a wee.

Everyone roared with laughter. I tried to shuffle away from him but my legs got tangled up together. Before I could stop myself, I was tumbling backwards, rolling along the catwalk and crashing three feet to the floor with a *thunk*.

I didn't get any sympathy from Rosie, though.

The hall lights came on and the next thing I knew she was looking down at me, her face a mask of fury. 'What do you think you're doing, you complete turdhead? Are you trying to ruin my entire life or wh—'

But she didn't finish because something unbelievable had happened. The rest of the class stopped laughing. Someone wolfwhistled. A group of people went: '*Oooh*.' And Mrs McDonald said, 'Wow! What an incredible outfit, Rosie.' By the time I'd struggled to my feet, everyone in the room was stamping their feet and cheering and clapping her. They thought she looked *good*! And Rosie was bowing and curtseying and pretending it was all a big surprise.

This was the weirdest thing that I'd ever seen.

Up until then anyway.

Things were about to get a whole lot weirder.

After School

When Grandma Hit the Deck

Rosie was utterly unbearable for the rest of the day. Everyone went mad for her crazy clothes. I had no idea why: to me, she'd looked like a complete weirdo. Everyone had loved it though. After she'd finished milking the applause, the fashion show had gone on for another twenty minutes. This was entirely made up of Rosie strutting around in her strange nature-based outfits (including 'sand dune' – a trouser suit made of sandpaper, topped off with a green spiky hat; and 'dream bird', which was a black feathery jacket that made her look like a really bad ostrich). The worst thing was that she insisted on me being onstage the whole time, stuck in my uncomfortable tree costume.

Eventually, Mrs McDonald had to step in and say we couldn't take any more excitement. Amazingly, she wasn't even being sarcastic when she said this. I thought at the time that Rosie was going to be cross, but she wasn't. In fact, she looked very pleased with herself indeed, like a penguin that'd hidden a fish under its tummy flap. Come to think of it, for all I knew, that could've been her next outfit.

Stranded Tortoise

The afternoon was bad enough but after school I had other things to think about. Like Grandma seeing the sleeveless crumper. I'd kind of forgotten about it because of the fashion show. But once I'd put it back on afterwards, I'd begun to feel seriously worried again. Grandma was not going to be impressed.

I dragged my feet the whole way home. When I finally arrived, I was surprised to find Mum blocking the front door, facing into the house. Inside, Grandma was trying to get past her with a huge rucksack on her back. Neither of them noticed me at first. 'Just let me through,' Grandma grunted.

Mum had both her hands stretched across the front doorway. 'You're not going. I've told you. It's too dangerous for a woman of your age.'

'I'll be fine,' said Grandma, straining to get round her. 'There'll be loads of us camping outside the shopping centre. And anyway, I've got to get there early. I need to get a decent view.'

'Of what?' asked Mum. They still hadn't noticed me standing there.

'Roman meeting the princess in my jumper, of course,' said Grandma.

I looked down at the sleeveless crumper and bit my lip guiltily.

'Princess Lucy isn't coming for two days,' snapped Mum, before calling inside to Dad. 'Will you tell her, please?'

Dad was standing halfway up the stairs. I could just about see the bottom half of his body. He was wearing probably the second-worst item of clothing I'd ever seen: a pair of horrible woolly shorts – no, *hot pants* – that Grandma had knitted for him the night before. They were way too small and his white, skinny legs below were like two pieces of hairy spaghetti. He pulled the shorts down over his buttocks. 'Are you planning to take your knitting machine with you?' he asked Grandma.

'No. There won't be electricity. And my fingers are still too sore to hand-knit.'

'So, if you go, would you be able to knit anything else?' I could tell that Dad was weighing this up carefully.

'No.'

I could almost *hear* the smile in Dad's voice. 'In that case, I say let her go. She'll probably be fine. The fresh air will do her good. And I expect you'd like a break from all your knitting, wouldn't you, Betty?'

'Fresh air?' cried Mum. 'She's eighty-three. What about the muggers, and the cold and . . .'

At that moment, when Mum's attention was diverted upstairs to Dad, Grandma burst past her and barrelled straight into my chest. This caused her to rebound off me, and she ended up lying on the floor on her back, balanced on top of the rucksack like a stranded terrapin.

Mum and I helped her to her feet. 'Are you alright?' she asked.

'I'll be OK,' grumbled Grandma. Then her eyes flicked towards the crumper. She gasped in shock. 'What . . . *happened* to the sleeves?'

I scratched the back of my neck. 'Well, there was this badger . . .'

My voice trailed away.

Grandma looked like she was about to cry. 'It's ruined.'

Mum raised an eyebrow. 'You won't be able to camp out in town now,' she said thoughtfully. 'You'll need to stay here and make Roman some new sleeves.'

'Really?' I said. I was hoping someone might finally suggest throwing the crumper in the bin.

'And while you're at it,' said Mum, warming to the idea, 'maybe you could make him a matching hat, and maybe some Princess Lucy jogging bottoms.'

I huffed out my cheeks. 'No need. Honestly.'

'But . . . but . . .' said Grandma. Her shoulders were slumped now, like she'd given up on the idea of camping out.

'Why don't I take you inside for a nice cup of tea, then you can get started?' said Mum, leading Grandma inside. As she passed me she mouthed

'Thank you' to me, as though I'd done anything at all.

'KNITTED JOGGING BOTTOMS?!' I mouthed back at her angrily.

They're a Bit Warm

About half an hour later, Grandma was just about to go upstairs to work on the new sleeves when there was a knock on the door.

It was Gamble. He looked terrible. There were mucky streaks down his face where he'd been crying, dried snot had crusted across his nose and cheeks, his clothes were filthy and there were bloody scratches all over his arms and legs.

'Found your sleeves," he said, holding them out to me.

'They're a bit *warm*,' I said, taking them off him. They were also filthy and ragged in parts. 'Where were they?'

'Down my undies,' said Gamble, as though nothing could be more normal. 'Don't have any pockets.'

'No,' I said, dropping the sleeves to the floor like they were radioactive (which wasn't impossible when you consider where they'd been). 'I meant, how did you find them? And what happened to you?'

At that point, Grandma shuffled up behind me. 'Oh wonderful!' she exclaimed, suddenly more cheerful as she saw the sleeves on the floor. 'I'll be able to fix the jumper much more easily now! It'll be as good as new in no time.'

I tried to smile as she scooped them up and rushed upstairs. *Brilliant.* It was bad enough when she was going to make new ones. Now I was going to have Gamble's underpant diseases all over my arms.

Gamble wiped his nose on his hand, which reminded me that he was upset. 'I went back to that wildlife place straight after school. Jumped the fence and crawled down one of the badger holes.'

This made me feel very uneasy. 'Why did you do that?'

Gamble shrugged. 'Felt bad about your jumper. You're my mate, innit? Anyway, I saw summat and it made me come up with a plan.'

'Oh,' I said. This *really* didn't sound good. The last time Gamble had a plan, he tried to make a taser out of a plug socket and a length of bare copper wire. I decided to change the subject. 'How did you get cut so badly?'

'Most of the badgers were pretty much asleep but one of 'em put up a fight.'

'Is that why you've been crying?'

'No!' he snapped, 'Gamble's don't cry, innit. I got grit in my eye.'

'Alright, calm down,' I said, holding up my palms. 'Just seeing if you were OK.'

There was a pause. Then he sniffed. 'Well, alright, so maybe I did cry a bit. You remember that badger with the bad back legs? Hoppalong.'

I nodded.

'Well, I was just crawling out of the hole and I heard voices. I had to hide. That Sue was chatting to some bloke outside the fence and saying Hoppalong's legs were worse and it'd taken him ages to go back down the hole after he'd come up this afternoon . . .' His voice tailed off.

My skin felt prickly. I wasn't sure I liked this. 'And?'

'If he doesn't improve by the weekend, they're gonna put him down!' Gamble screamed, before suddenly exploding in a massive burst of snot and tears. 'And . . . and . . . it made me feel bad cos it's all my fault she saw him like that . . . and if they put him down just cos he ain't much good any more then what if someone puts me down too . . . ?'

He flung his arms round me, soaking my shoulder. He felt all wet and bony and, from the smell of him, I was fairly sure he might not have had a shower since the canal incident. It was like being hugged by a half-starved otter.

Holding my breath, I eased his arms off me. 'I'm sure nobody will put you down. Or Hoppalong.'

'They will,' sobbed Gamble, his bottom lip sticking out and wobbling. 'All the times I've been mean to animals. It just made me think. I've got to do something, Roman. I've got to. I owe it to Hoppalong. And I owe it to the princess.'

With that he turned round and ran away down the street.

THURSDAY

Morning

When Problems Came Down from the Sky

I was worried when I got into the classroom on Thursday morning because there was no sign of Gamble anywhere. *Where was he?* I hated to think of what he might be doing, particularly considering how upset he'd been. He's so unpredictable. I remembered the time he'd nicked off school and run away to Australia to become a professional didgeridoo player. The coastguard had rescued him floating out to sea on a rubber ring. The only supplies he'd had were a lump of cheese and a homemade 'whacking stick' in case of a shark attack.

My thoughts were interrupted by Rosie Taylor's

smarmy voice. 'Wow. Just when I thought that the crumper couldn't get any worse . . .'

I ground my teeth together. Overnight, Grandma had sewn the sleeves back on. Unfortunately they were now completely frayed where the badgers had been chewing them. Plus they stank of badger (a smell I've never experienced before – a cross between rotten fruit and abandoned toilets). *Plus*, Grandma had sewn them on really badly so they were painfully tight around my shoulders. And to make things worse, she'd tried to make it look 'trendy and modern' by sewing a line of sequins from the elbows to the wrists. In short, I looked more ridiculous than ever.

Gamble didn't show up all day. Wherever he'd got to, though, it wasn't like he missed a great deal in school: all we did was make welcome signs for Princess Lucy. This is the kind of lame-o lesson that teachers always come up with when they can't think of anything proper to do. Some people really went to town on theirs – glitter, gel pens, shiny stickers, the works. Predictably, mine was rubbish. It looked like a baby elephant with a twitch had got a few felt tips stuck up its trunk and tripped up onto a piece of paper.

At lunchtime a few people carried out their last attempts at raising money for the badger charity.

Vanya did her sponsored run – she went round and round the field for the whole hour without stopping, which was mega-impressive. A couple of girls did a sponsored silence, and Kevin '*Ali Blargh Blargh and the Forty Heaves*' Harrison got people to throw wet sponges at him for ten pence a go. By now though, I'd kind of given up on the fundraising. I was happy to sponsor a couple of other people, cheer Vanya on and chuck some sponges at Kevin (until one hit him in the belly and he had to go and throw up) but I thought it was pretty unlikely that Vanya and I would raise enough to meet the princess ourselves. In any case, I think that the two hundred pounds for the sponsored crumper-wearing was pretty impressive, even if it didn't count towards my total.

At the end of the afternoon, Mrs McDonald spoke to the whole class about meeting Princess Lucy the next day. 'There'll be a coach in the morning. Don't be late, whatever you do. You're representing the school so look smart.'

At this, Rosie burst out laughing. 'Yeah, Roman. Good luck with that!'

Mrs McDonald ignored her. 'So, we've counted up all the sponsorship money – over five hundred pounds by the way, so well done!'

Everyone clapped.

'And now I'll tell you which three lucky people will be meeting Princess Lucy tomorrow.'

The classroom fell into silence. I wasn't particularly bothered. I mean, there was no way *I* was going to be meeting her – I'd hardly raised anything. And anyway, I didn't really want to draw any more attention to myself when I was already going to be wearing the crumper.

A lot of other people were nervously biting their lips and crossing their fingers. 'In no particular order,' continued Mrs McDonald, 'it will be Rosie . . .'

Even though I was expecting this, I groaned inwardly.

Rosie stood up. 'Thank you, fans,' she said, even though nobody was clapping. 'When the princess and I become friends I will never forget you.' She paused. 'I mean, obviously I'll never talk to you again because I won't be allowed to mix with commoners, and if you come anywhere near me I'll probably have you arrested or maybe even shot. But still, you'll always have a place in my heart.'

'And Vanya . . .' said Mrs McDonald when Rosie had finally sat down. Vanya gave a fist pump and I high-fived her. I felt so happy for her. This was ace news – she was going to meet the princess.

'And . . .' continued Mrs McDonald, dramatically. A few people did a drumroll on the desks.

'Stop!' announced Rosie.

Mrs McDonald looked over her glasses at her. 'Is everything OK?'

'I've made a decision,' Rosie said. Her voice was slow and soft, like the sound of a snake sliding up your trouser leg. 'I'm going to donate half of the money I earned to Roman.'

'What?!' I said, my eyes bursting out of my head. Rosie was being *nice* to me? This was literally the last thing in the world I was expecting. Honestly, I'd have been less surprised if Princess Lucy had pogo-sticked into the room dressed as the Easter Bunny and given me a pet unicorn.

'Are you sure?' asked Mrs McDonald.

'Positive!' said Rosie, smiling sweetly. 'After all, Roman has worn his crumper all week and not a single penny has gone to his total. I feel *really guilty.*'

'Well, thank you, Rosie. How kind,' said Mrs McDonald.

Hmmm. *Guilty?* What was it about this that made me suspicious? Well, maybe the fact that Rosie had never felt guilty in her life; not even that time when she spread that rumour round school that my butt cheeks were covered in long, white hair 'like a wizard's beard'.

Still, whatever her reasons, this did mean one thing, which became clear as Miss Clegg altered the totals on the fundraising chart.

And of course, because my total had been increased, this also meant that . . .

'Nice one, Roman! We're going to meet Princess Lucy together!' Vanya cried, giving me a massive hug. A couple of people half-heartedly clapped even though they looked disappointed themselves.

'As long as you wear the crumper,' said Rosie. I tried to ignore this, but I had a sneaking feeling that Rosie was planning something.

'So, Rosie, Roman and Vanya, you three will give the princess her flowers,' Mrs McDonald said. 'Everyone else, we'll wave our signs from the sides and cheer them on.'

I sat there unsure of what to think. I mean, on the one hand it was going to be pretty amazing to meet a real princess, and Grandma would be totally over the moon. But I'd still be wearing the crumper. And now all eyes would be on me.

Little did I know that, by Friday, the crumper would be the least of my worries.

Buzzing

Because I wasn't walking home with Gamble, and Vanya had karate after school, I decided to take a shortcut home across the park. I had fifty pence in my pocket and I reckoned I should nip into Gibson's and buy a jam doughnut to celebrate being chosen to meet the princess. I mean, I had plenty of doubts about it but still, any excuse to have a doughnut.

I was about halfway across when I heard my name being called from behind me. *Rosie*. Hmmm.

Wearily, I turned round to face her. 'Are you OK?'

Rosie tottered right up on her high heels. 'Aren't you going to thank me properly, Roman?'

I huffed out my cheeks. 'Thanks. I guess. It was pretty kind of you.'

She sniggered. 'Yes. Of course. Kind.'

'What do you mean?' I asked, my eyes narrowing.

She licked her lips. 'Don't you want to know why I chose you?'

The simple answer to this was that I didn't really care. But I didn't reply because there was a funny mechanical buzzing noise coming from the bush behind her. Before I could see what was causing it, though, she'd stamped on my foot.

'Ow!' I said, wincing.

'Listen to me when I'm talking to you!' Rosie snapped. Then she gave a nasty smile. 'It was all because of the fashion show, if you must know.'

'Why are you telling me this?' I asked, trying to get away from her.

She grabbed my wrist. 'Because I don't want you to think for even a millisecond that I did it because I like you.'

The buzzing noise got louder. At first I thought it might be a lawnmower. But it was too quiet and high-pitched for that, and suddenly it seemed to be higher off the ground, coming from behind the very top of the bush.

'Well, that's nice,' I said, 'but can you please let go of my arm? I want to go and buy a doughnut.'

Rosie didn't seem to hear me. Her face was twisted and cruel. Red splotches were growing on her cheeks as she dug her nails painfully into my arm. 'Do you realise how long I've dreamed of being a princess? This is my big chance! I need it. And you're going to help me.'

'How?'

'Oh, Roman. You remember my blog, don't you? Rule four? "You might like to have at least one ugly friend. That way you'll always look better when you're with them."'

I remembered reading the words. *Typical Rosie.*

She carried on talking, her voice becoming more excited with every word. 'I *need* you. You're such a freak you'll make me look even better in front of the princess. You heard everyone cheering at the fashion show, didn't you? They weren't cheering just for me – though I did look amaaaaaazing, of course. No. I realised afterwards that they cheered for me because *you* looked so abysmal that you made me look even more gorge-alicious than I already am.'

I rolled my eyes. *I might've known.*

'And because Princess Lucy didn't show up yesterday, it means that I've only got one chance to impress her and become her BFF and personal fashion adviser . . .'

I'd basically stopped listening to her by this point. The buzzing had continued to get louder and higher. I had to squint against the sun but I swear that just above the bush I could see something hovering in the air. A helicopter? A UFO? It disappeared again almost immediately and I glanced back at Rosie.

'. . . so tomorrow,' she continued, '*you* will make me look even more fashionable and perfect because you'll be wearing the crumper.'

She said 'crumper' like she was actually saying 'used bum flannel'. I'm not actually sure if that would've been worse or not.

'And what if I don't want to?' I asked, briefly looking away from the top of the bush.

Rosie half smiled. 'If you dare to spoil my chances tomorrow I swear I'll have your insides scooped out and . . .'

Just then a shadow was cast on the ground behind Rosie. Above the bush rose the unmistakable sight of Spud Gamble's drone. It was dipping and weaving crazily from side to side, and sparks were spitting out beneath it. At first I thought it was broken or on fire but then I realised that the robotic arm underneath it seemed to be carrying a sparkler – you know, the kind you hold on Bonfire Night. The drone swung from side to side in a strange jerky pattern. What on earth was going on?

Meanwhile, Rosie was still yakking away at me. 'I've been through hell this week just so I can meet the princess.'

'Have you?'

'Yes! And I'm not going to let it all be for nothing just because of you. I've had to raise money for stinking, disgusting animals.' She seemed unaware that the drone was now swirling around directly above her head, sparks landing on the ground behind her. 'Do you know how sick that makes me feel? I *hate* animals. I don't want to keep them safe. They're almost as vile as you! If I could, I'd line up every badger in Britain and run them over in Daddy's Range Rover. In fact . . .' She suddenly looked upwards. 'What is th—'

She didn't get the chance to finish because, at that moment, something really, really terrible happened.

Something Really, Really Terrible

It was awful.

The drone just *stopped* in mid-air as though someone had pressed pause on it. Then, before I could dodge out of the way, it plunged downwards like a rock, straight at us. I screwed my eyes up and tensed my whole body. But the impact never came. I felt it whoosh above me, skimming the top of my head.

Then there was a loud *clunk*.

Rosie screamed.

I opened one eye. Rosie had been knocked flat on her back, and the huge drone was upside down on top of her. The last few sparks were still sputtering out of the sparkler.

'Rosie! Are you hurt?' I cried. Even though I can't stand her I felt like I had to help. I tried to lift the drone off her but it wouldn't budge. 'Is it your head?'

'It's much worse than that, you complete donkey's rectum!' wailed Rosie, which told me she was probably OK. 'It's my *hair*!'

Up close I could see that Rosie's hair was completely tangled up in the propellers of the drone. I was just wondering whether this was really bad or really funny when I noticed a strange smell.

Burning?!

I looked down at my arms and chest.

Oh nuggets!

I was on fire.

I was so worried about Rosie that I hadn't even realised. It must've been the sparkler. Flames were creeping up my arms. I tried to slap at them but within seconds they were out of control and my skin was starting to sting. Quick as a flash I tried to whip the crumper off but my head caught in the tight neck hole. The flames had spread. I was burning alive. With a final surge of adrenalin, I yanked it off and flung it away from me. By the time it landed on the grass it was an absolute inferno. *Good grief,* I thought. *What did Grandma use to make it? Petrol-soaked wool?*

At that moment, Gamble came round the corner of the bush. He was followed by his brother Spud, who was having a go at him. 'You've got to be gentler with the controls, our Darren. If you've bust it I'll . . . oh-oh!'

'What's going on?' I asked breathlessly. 'You nearly killed me!'

Gamble grinned. 'It's my big plan. I'm gonna take the drone to town tomorrow. Then, when the princess arrives, I'm gonna write *Save Hoppalong* in the sky using a sparkler, innit? Then maybe she'll stop the wildlife hospital from putting him down and I won't feel so bad about all the things I've done to animals. Anyway – what's up with you?'

'Your sparkler set me on fire!'

'That is so cool,' replied Gamble. 'I'd *love* to be set on fire.'

I was about to say that this definitely was *not*

cool when Rosie interrupted. 'Stop thinking about yourself all the time, Roman. My hair is in trouble here, people. My *hair*. And if someone doesn't help me out soon then I am gonna have a major freakout.'

'Calm down. I'll get you out,' sniffed Spud.

Then, before she could say anything, he'd pulled a penknife out of his pocket, lifted up the drone and calmly sliced through her tangled hair. He did it so quickly that Rosie didn't have time to stop him.

'Done!' He grinned. 'No need to thank me.'

I thought it was unlikely that Rosie would thank him any time soon. Her face was frozen in shock. Her hand slowly rose to her head and patted around where her hair used to be. Then she made a noise like a stranded baby rabbit.

'Quality hairdo,' said Darren, flipping the drone off her and inspecting his brother's handiwork. 'You look like the lead singer of Dr Lunatic and the Mental Patients.'

I'm no expert on hair but I was sure of one thing: 'quality' wasn't the word I'd have used to describe it. Rosie's hair was normal at the sides, but down the centre was a wide strip where it was short and spiky. It looked like one of those aeroplane runways that've been cut through the jungle. The haircut was so terrible that I'd forgotten all about the crumper, which was now little more than a pile of smouldering ashes.

Finally, Rosie regained the power of speech. 'WHATHAVEYOUDONE?!' she wailed, leaping to her feet.

Emergency

Rosie was straight on the phone. Her cheeks were blotchy and her eye was flickering like crazy. 'I need an ambulance! Now!'

There was a short pause while the person at the other end spoke.

Rosie's face had gone purple and she was completely losing it. *'Twenty minutes?!* How do you expect me to wait that long? It's an emergency, you useless buffoon.'

Another pause.

'No, I DON'T need to go to hospital!' she bellowed, pacing up and down frantically. 'It's far more important than that. I need to go to my **hairdresser!'**

Wow! I thought. Even by Rosie's standards, this was pretty extreme. She continued jabbering into the phone. 'What do you mean *time-wasting*? Who are these *other people* with *serious injuries*? Don't you know who I am?'

I'm guessing that at this point the operator said 'no' because Rosie went bananas.

'I'm *hashtag* Rosie Taylor, for heaven's sake. I'm a style icon. And if this doesn't get sorted out soon then I'll end up meeting royalty tomorrow looking like I've just had an argument with a lawnmower.'

I could tell that the operator was trying to talk but Rosie had hit her stride. 'Now you get on the radio right now and tell those jumped-up bus drivers to tip out whoever's in the back of their ambulances and get here right now because when Rosie Taylor becomes friends with Princess Lucy, Rosie Taylor swears that she'll . . .'

Rosie pulled the phone away from her ear and looked at it in disgust and disbelief. 'She hung up on me. *Me?!* The nerve of it.'

Then she turned to face me.

And that was when I laughed.

I didn't mean to, and I shouldn't have done, and I know it wasn't nice.

But I couldn't help myself. She just looked *so* ridiculous, standing there like a really angry coconut.

'How dare you laugh at me!' she snarled. 'This is all your fault, Roman!'

I stopped laughing immediately. 'How?'

'If it wasn't for you and your stupid crumper, I wouldn't have sponsored you, then I wouldn't have given you all the money for it. So I wouldn't have been standing here at all and this little tramp wouldn't have ruined my beautiful hair.'

'But . . .' I began. It all sounded a bit complicated to me. And anyway – I hadn't asked her to sponsor me, or to follow me across the park. And I certainly couldn't be blamed for Gamble going crazy with the drone.

'She's got a point,' sniffed Gamble. 'Apart from the bit about me being a tramp.'

Strangely enough, this was the only part of what she'd said that I *did* think she had a point about.

Rosie's eyes narrowed. 'Oh, you just wait, Roman,' she said. 'Once I've called my dad and got this mess sorted out, I'm going to get you back for this.'

She pulled a silk scarf out of her handbag and

tied it round her head. Then she turned and stormed off across the park.

I hurried off in the opposite direction, leaving Gamble, Spud and my burned-up crumper behind me.

Depressed

Back at home, Grandma took the news about the blazing crumper pretty badly.

'How could you, Roman?' she whined. 'Such a beautiful jumper.'

'I had to get it off,' I explained. 'I could've been roasted like a turkey.'

Grandma didn't seem to hear me. 'Imagine how wonderful it would've been to see my grandson standing before the princess in one of my creations. It would've been the greatest moment of my life. I'm heartbroken. Heartbroken.'

Her whole body sagged like a dropped beanbag.

I felt totally sorry for her, even though I have to say I was delighted that the crumper was no longer in existence. 'Well, at least you'll still get to see the princess,' I said, trying to cheer her up. 'You love the princess, Grandma.'

'Huh,' said Grandma, slouching down on the sofa. 'But you won't be wearing the jumper. What's the point in going? It's like being told you're going to have a box of chocolates then just being given the box instead.'

She reached to the table by the side of the sofa, where she had a set of knitting needles and a ball of wool. After a few half-hearted stiches, she huffed out her cheeks and dropped the lot into the bin.

I felt terrible.

It was then that the doorbell rang.

New Lease of Life

I opened the front door and nearly fell over. Rosie Taylor – the worst person in the world ever – was standing on my doorstep, a large leather handbag over her shoulder. Behind her on the street, her dad's shiny black Range Rover was parked up, engine purring.

'Two mins, Daddy,' Rosie called, waving towards the car. Then she pushed right past me and into the house. Her hair had been cut short all over and slicked down flat against her scalp. This made her head look *tiny* – even smaller than Gamble's. From behind it looked like she was balancing a rabbit dropping on her neck.

'Yeah, I know,' she said, smoothing down her side parting. 'It's a pretty drastic cut but my personal stylist Antonio just said go for it. Be fearless.'

'Fascinating,' I said.

Rosie didn't notice the sarcasm in my voice. 'I based it on that Swedish singer Ulrika Klogg. I put a photo of it out there on Instagram and I've already got, *like,* three thousand likes, which is, *like,* a lot of likes.'

'Amazing,' I said. 'Why are you calling round for me?'

Rosie clicked her fingers in front of my face to shut me up. 'Oh, puuurrrleaase. As if I've come here to see a weird little dweeblet like you! Hashtag: in your dreams.'

'Then who?'

'The old crone of course. Get her now,' she snapped. Then she looked around her in disgust, like she'd woken up and found herself in a cave made entirely out of earwax. 'I'd rather not spend any more time than I have to in this dreadful hovel.'

At that moment, Grandma shuffled into the hall.

Rosie's face immediately lit up. 'Oh hello. How lovely to see you again.'

Grandma forced a smile.

'OMG,' said Rosie, patting Grandma on the head like she was a prize poodle. 'Can I just say, I loooooved that jumper you made for Roman. It was fabalicious.'

'Didn't you call it a *crumper*?' I said.

'Yeah – as in a crazy-*cool* jumper,' tutted Rosie.

'Well. It doesn't matter now anyway,' said Grandma, sounding depressed. 'It's gone forever.'

'Tell me about it. What a tragicalamity for the world of fashion,' said Rosie, shaking her head. 'I literally cried so hard that I thought my eyes would fall out. I was *so* much looking forward to Princess Lucy and the world's cameras seeing Roman wearing it.' She paused and leaned forward to Grandma. 'But maybe it isn't *all* gone.'

Reaching into her handbag, she pulled out a small square of black, burned material, about the size of a birthday card.

A chill shot up and down my spine. 'What's that?'

Rosie smiled smugly. 'After Antonio had saved my hair I thought that I should save your crumper. So I sent Daddy back to the park to rescue it.'

'Why would you do that?' I asked.

Ignoring me, Rosie turned to Grandma. 'Do you have your knitting machine with you?'

'Well . . . yes,' said Grandma.

'Oh goody gumdrops,' said Rosie, holding up her handbag. 'I've found you a pattern on the internet and Daddy got me some wool from the craft store in his shopping centre. Take me to the machine and I'll reveal everything.'

I didn't like the sound of this one bit. 'What are you doing?'

Rosie dropped her voice so that Grandma couldn't hear her. 'Oh, Roman, you didn't think Daddy would let you off wearing the crumper just because it was destroyed, did you? Of course he'll expect you to honour your promise. Otherwise he won't give the money to charity. Then the blood of a thousand badgers will be on your hands and I'll have to tell the princess. You wouldn't want that, would you? So if you don't mind . . .'

She led Grandma towards the stairs. I went to follow them but Rosie blocked me off. 'Oh no no no. You can't see it until tomorrow. It'll ruin the surprise.'

'How exciting!' said Grandma, who'd completely

cheered up. She shuffled up after Rosie, leaving me behind.

As they reached the top of the stairs, Rosie turned back and gave me an ice-cold smile; the kind of smile a man-eating kangaroo might give you just before jumping up and down on your head.

I gulped.

Second Visitor

They'd only just disappeared into Grandma's bedroom when a second person knocked on the door. Before I'd even opened it, I realised it was Gamble.

I knew it was him because when I reached the front door, I saw a pair of skinny bare buttocks pressed against the entrance hall window. *Disgusting*.

I opened the door. Thankfully Gamble had pulled up his trousers. He was dressed all in black and he had something under his arm.

'Isn't that Mrs McDonald's guinea pig cage?' I asked.

Gamble grinned. 'Yep. I nipped back into school after I saw you at the park and she lent it to me.'

I raised my eyebrow.

'Alright, so she doesn't know she's lent it to me,'

he sniffed. 'I'll give it back, though. I only need it tonight.'

'What for?'

Gamble tapped the side of his nose. 'Can't say anything now. Secret plan, innit? I'm not gonna do the sparkler thing any more. It's too dangerous.'

Gamble isn't normally worried about danger. One time he brought his dad's chainsaw into class because, and I quote, 'The pencil sharpeners here are well rubbish.' Luckily Miss Clegg sat on him to pin him down before he could use it.

'What are you going to do?' I asked. I had a terrible feeling that I already knew the answer to this but I was *really* hoping I was wrong.

'I'll tell you when we get there. Come on.'

'No, I can't. I was about to go to bed,' I said, even though it was only seven o'clock and I hadn't even put on the knitted pyjamas Grandma had made me yet. 'Where are you going?'

Gamble's head twitched about like he was worried someone might be following him. 'Somewhere. You not gonna help then?'

'Sorry. Too late,' I said. Even if it had been the middle of the day I wouldn't have gone with him, though. It's never good when Gamble acts secretively.

Who could forget the time when he kidnapped Kevin 'Ali Blargh Blargh and the Forty Heaves' Harrison, shoved him in a box and tried to post him to New Zealand? He only got caught when the people at the post office saw the sick leaking out of the bottom of the parcel. 'Can't you ask your brother?'

Gamble sniffed. 'Nah. Spud's been sacked from the bakery. He's had to go back to pinching stuff instead.'

'Sacked?' I said, feeling really uneasy and trying not to think about the second part of what he'd just said. 'What did he do?'

'It was well unfair,' sighed Gamble, 'all he did was take a pork pie home with him.'

'And they sacked him for that?' I said. Even though Spud is clearly even more of a nutter than Darren, this didn't exactly seem worth losing his job over.

Gamble moved some dust around on the floor with his huge clompy boots. 'Well. I mean, it *was* an absolutely massive one.'

'Oh,' I said.

'And he *did* empty out all of the meat from it and leave it on the floor of the kitchen before he took it.'

'Right.'

'And after he'd done that he *did* kind of stuff the pastry full of money from the till.'

'OK.'

'And he might've got away with it if he hadn't beaten up the manager with his own shoes afterwards.'

'Good grief,' I said. There was an awkward pause, then I yawned to show him that I *really* wanted this conversation to end.

For once, Gamble took the hint. 'I'm off then. Thought you might wanna help after all the trouble your jumper caused, but never mind. I'll manage, innit. I'll see you in town tomorrow.'

He gave me a 'friendly' punch in the arm then walked off.

'Hang on,' I called after him, 'I thought you were banned from meeting the princess?'

Gamble didn't turn round. 'Banned from going *with school*,' he said over his shoulder. 'But it's a free country, innit? They can't stop me from nicking off, can they?'

'I'm not sure about that . . .' I said, but he'd already disappeared from sight.

One thing was clear, though – just because the crumper had been destroyed, it wasn't going to stop ruining my life.

FRIDAY

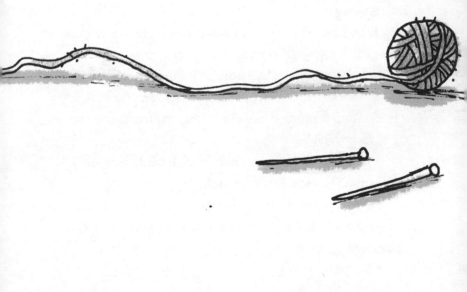

The Royal Visit

When Princess Lucy Came to Town and Gamble Caused a Major Incident

I found it really hard to sleep on Thursday night, for six reasons:

1) The constant clattering of Grandma's knitting machine, which went on late into the night. This was made worse by . . .

↓

2) My 'bed'. I'd ditched the popped inflatable mattress a few days ago, so now I was trying to sleep on an old pile of coats on the floor. This was about as comfortable

as falling down the stairs. Not being able to sleep made me worry even more about . . .

↓

3) Meeting Princess Lucy. OK, so it was obviously going to be pretty cool to meet a real-life royal, and I'd have Vanya with me, but it was also seriously nerve-wracking. My mind was racing with all the stupid things I could end up doing. What if I broke wind, or accidentally headbutted her, or wet myself? These thoughts were made worse by . . .

↓

4) The fear of what *exactly* it could be that Grandma was knitting. The TV cameras and local newspapers were going to be there – imagine if pictures of me wearing something even worse than the crumper were beamed around the globe. I'd never be allowed to forget it. Which brings me to . . .

↓

5) Rosie. She'd stayed in Grandma's room for twenty minutes. When she'd left the house afterwards, she'd slapped me lightly on the cheek three times and told me that she 'couldn't wait to see me the next day'. Then she'd swanned off back to her dad's car, cackling like an evil witch. And if all *that* wasn't bad enough, I still had to worry about . . .

6) Gamble. What on earth was he planning? I mean, I was pretty certain that I knew what he was up to but I was hoping he wasn't going to do it. Surely he couldn't be that crazy . . . could he?

Well, it turned out that what he did was worse than anything I could've imagined. Sadly, though, there were many other terrible things that happened first.

I reckon I'd had about an hour's sleep when Mum dragged the covers off my 'bed'. 'Today's your big day!' she sang, pulling open the curtains.

I rubbed my eyes and looked at my clock. 'This is ridiculous, Mum. It's half six! In the morning!

This is child cruelty. What are you going to do next? Pull out my fingernails?'

Mum ignored me. 'Got to be at school early for the bus, remember?'

'Urgh. How could I forget?' I grunted, dragging myself out of bed and downstairs.

Grandma was sitting in the kitchen, slurping a cup of tea. There was a plastic bag by her feet, which appeared to be stuffed with something. Something large and soft and *knitted*. I reached out to have a look at it but Grandma pulled it away.

'Oh no you don't!' she smiled. 'That lovely girl Rosie said you weren't to see it till she got here.'

Lovely? This was Rosie Taylor she was talking about: a girl who once told everyone in our class that I'm 'still not toilet-trained', and that she saw my mum 'changing my bot-bot' in the café at Sainsbury's.

At that moment the doorbell rang. Rosie strode into the house before I could reach the door. She was wearing a long sparkly ballgown and loads of jewellery. Her short hair was slapped down with so much gunky gel that she looked like a seagull that'd been rescued from an oil slick.

As she tottered into the hall on her ludicrous

high heels, she noticed me staring. 'Yeah. I look amazing, don't I? I've been up since two o'clock this morning.'

'Why would you do that?' I asked.

'OMG Roman,' she tutted, jutting out her lower jaw. 'You really are dumb, aren't you? Do you have any *idea* how important today is? This is literally my only chance to become a princess. If *you* are going to look a hundred per cent bad, *I've* got to look a hundred per cent perfect.'

Rosie swept past me and into the kitchen. 'Have you finished it?' she demanded when she saw Grandma.

In reply, Grandma waggled the plastic bag at her.

'Right then, Roman,' said Rosie. 'Time to try on your outfit for meeting the princess . . .'

The Outfit

So, earlier, I might've mentioned that the crumper was the worst item of clothing in the world ever.

I lied.

The new outfit Grandma had knitted for me made the crumper look like an edible sweatshirt made out of actual doughnuts.

Let me try to explain: wearing the crumper was like being beaten up by a three-year-old – quite painful and pretty embarrassing. Wearing this horrific new outfit was like being attacked with a cheese grater while standing in front of the whole school in the nude – excruciating and humiliating.

Grandma had knitted me a woolly badger onesie.

Yep, as in a onesie that looked like a badger.

It was grey on the back and black on the front, and it had a black-and-white stripy hood with little ears and a pointy nose sticking out. It was so warm that I was only able to wear my undies underneath it.

'Can I take it off now?' I said, immediately after Grandma and Rosie had forced me into it.

'No chance,' said Rosie, snapping away with her camera phone. 'You were sponsored, remember.'

'No,' I said. 'I was sponsored to wear the jumper.'

'But this *is* the jumper,' said Grandma, pointing to a little patch on my chest. 'What's left of it, anyway.'

I looked down. Sewn into the front of the onesie was a small square of black, burned wool. I recognised it as the remaining piece of the crumper that Rosie had brought round yesterday. Grandma had obviously sewn it in a rush – a strand of thread about five centimetres long was dangling down off it.

I reached down to snap off the thread and Grandma slapped my hand away. 'Don't do that! You'll pull out all the stitches.'

Rosie gave one of her little slug's bum smiles. 'Now, since the crumper no longer exists in its previous form, you *have* to wear this, Roman. For the sake of those poor innocent badgers.'

'You said you hated badgers,' I growled.

'You can't prove that,' said Rosie, pretending to look shocked. 'In any case, if you take this off you'll have broken your promise. And you know what my daddy will do if you break a promise to him.'

Feeling uneasy, I tugged on the back of the onesie where it'd ridden up between my bum cheeks.

'Now,' said Grandma, clapping her podgy little hands together. 'Let's go and see this princess . . .'

Excitement

Dad had taken the morning off work for the princess's visit, so he dropped me at school then drove on to town with Grandma and Mum afterwards. Rosie hopped in with us. Normally she wouldn't be seen dead in an old banger like Dad's but I think she wanted to make sure I didn't take off the onesie.

'What a charming little car,' she said, as she squashed in the back with Mum and me. I don't think she meant this, though – she *did* insist that Dad covered the seats with plastic sheets before she'd get in. 'I love it. It's like going back in time to find out how poor people used to live. You know, before cars were good.'

'Thanks,' said Dad. 'I think.'

When we arrived, Dad dropped us off and we went straight to the coach. Most of our class were already on board, bouncing around with excitement. Rosie pushed on in front of me and grabbed the driver's microphone: 'And now, ladies and gentleman,' she announced, as I wearily climbed the stairs behind her. 'Putting the *bad* into badger – it's Roman!'

When they saw me, everyone stood up, pointing and hooting and laughing at me like a bunch of chimpanzees.

'Haha!' sniggered Miss Clegg, who was ticking names off on the register. She seemed a lot happier without Darren to look after. 'What *do* you look like?'

She could talk, by the way. She was wearing a skin-tight red dress. I'm not sure that it was meant to be skin-tight, though. I don't want to be cruel but Miss Clegg is a little bit overweight. The dress looked like a novelty balloon filled with custard.

'Well, I think you look *wonderful*,' said Mrs McDonald, who was sitting next to her. If possible, her clothes were even worse. She was wearing a bright green dress with little triangular Union Jacks hanging off it. She looked like she'd been mummified in bunting. 'So cute.'

I smiled weakly. As I made my way down the bus, Rosie continued her 'hilarious' commentary on the microphone. 'Like all badgers,' she said, 'Roman stinks, he has a brain the size of an apple, he lives in a disgusting hole in the ground and he's crawling with fleas.'

Grinding my teeth together, I sat down next to Vanya, who gave me a friendly grin. 'Don't listen to her. I think you look cool,' she said. This was a nice thing to say but she *was* laughing at the time so I didn't know if I could believe her.

Of course, there was no Gamble on the coach, and I tried not to think about what he might've been up to since leaving my house the night before.

Also, Kevin 'Ali Blargh Blargh and the Forty Heaves' Harrison was walking to the shopping centre with his parents so he didn't get travel sick. As a result, at least I didn't have to worry about anything being thrown at me or thrown up on me and I was able to look out of the window the whole way into town.

Passing through the streets, I couldn't believe how enthusiastic everyone seemed to be. There were enormous crowds lining the pavements. People were waving British flags, market traders were flogging Princess Lucy T-shirts and tea towels, police officers were strolling up and down the barriers keeping an eye on everyone.

The closer we got to town, the bigger the crowds – maybe four or five deep behind the barriers. Some of the people had clearly slept there overnight. Massive trucks from the TV companies were parked in the side streets. When we got close to the shopping centre, the road was closed and the driver had to show a special pass so that the police would let him through to drop us off. The only people in the road were a couple of reporters speaking into TV cameras.

My belly swirled like a whirlpool of nerves and

excitement. I was about to meet a princess. This was a seriously big deal.

And I was dressed as a badger.

I folded my arms and shuddered.

Not only did I look like an idiot, but I was also concerned about Gamble. Looking round the faces in the crowd, I think I was the only person in the whole town who wasn't completely and utterly, one hundred per cent happy.

Unfortunately for them, their happiness wouldn't last either.

Practice

The coach left us in the middle of the road outside the shopping centre. It was weird being in an open space surrounded by crowds. People were crammed onto both pavements, with a great big gap outside the shopping centre for Princess Lucy to enter through.

Opposite, a huddle of newspaper photographers and TV cameras were standing ready. Immediately, Rosie Taylor strode over and started posing and pouting in front of them.

'Can you move out of the way?' said one of

them. Rosie looked furious, which made me pleased. Well, for half a millisecond anyway, until the photographer continued: 'We need a couple of snaps of that short kid in the silly outfit.'

I guess he meant me.

Rosie pretended not to be upset as she tottered past me on her high heels. 'Pictures of freaks sell newspapers,' she said icily, 'but it'll be *me* they want when I'm besties with Princess Lucy.'

The cameras clicked at me and I forced a smile.

'Come on now, everyone!' said Mrs McDonald. 'This is so exciting!'

Glad to turn away from the flashes and clicking shutters, I followed her towards the shopping centre. People in the crowd noticed the costume and laughed. I was already sweating like mad under all that wool, but now I was blushing as well. Without wanting to get too personal, I was glad I was only wearing my pants underneath.

Outside the shopping centre, a whole bunch of workers were carrying out the final, frantic finishing touches. Street cleaners were scrubbing the flagstones while two more people rolled a long red carpet out from the front doors. Some men on ladders were stringing bunting between the lamp-posts. One woman even seemed to be spray-painting the flowers in the massive pots outside to make them look more pink. And there were police wandering around everywhere, looking suspiciously at everybody.

The police at least made me feel a bit calmer. I mean, if Gamble *did* show up and try something crazy, they'd be able to stop him straight away.

Wouldn't they?

At that moment, Rosie's dad stormed out of the shopping centre.

'Oi!' he called at one of the workmen on the ladder. 'Make sure that bunting isn't tangled. And *you* over there: if there's any chewing gum left on that flagstone I'll literally explode. And *you* with the brush – are you cleaning the kerb or tickling it? Useless idiots.'

When he'd finished shouting at everyone else, he turned to us.

'Good grief,' he said, puffing out his cheeks. 'Have they all got uglier or something?'

'Well . . .' spluttered Mrs McDonald.

Rosie's dad ran his hand through his hair. He looked extremely stressed out by the princess's visit. 'She'll be here in ten minutes. Too late to hire models now. We'll just have to keep the weird-looking ones away from the cameras. Ditch the welcome posters; they're way too tacky for a classy place like this, and I'm not having anything that could block out the name of the shopping centre on the TV.'

I didn't like Rosie's dad very much at all.

'But the posters look sweet,' protested Mrs McDonald, 'and the children worked so hard on them.'

'Did they?' asked Rosie's dad, looking very surprised. 'Wow! Doesn't look like it. Get rid.'

Once we'd hidden our posters in a store cupboard by the entrance, Rosie's dad noticed my badger outfit for the first time. He took a step backwards. 'Yikes! What on earth is that thing?! Looks like a coat you'd buy for a dog you didn't like. Take it off!'

'I want him to wear it, Daddy,' said Rosie. 'It's important.'

Rosie's dad sighed. 'OK, darling. If you insist.'

'And anyway! I made that!' called out Grandma from the crowd behind him.

Mr Taylor spun round. When he saw Grandma he made a face like he'd just trodden in something unpleasant. 'Not again,' he sighed, before clicking his fingers to get the attention of a policewoman who was standing nearby. 'Officer. I told you to dispose of all the homeless people.'

Dispose of them? I thought. That didn't sound very nice. And anyway, *homeless*? I mean, Grandma *was* wearing her self-knitted pink cardigan which was all misshapen and tatty but still, I thought this was pretty harsh.

'You can't *dispose* of homeless people,' said Vanya angrily. 'They're not mouldy tomatoes; they're human beings.'

'That's debatable,' said Rosie's dad, 'but anyway, the princess will be here soon. We can't have *vagrants* spreading their germs everywhere.'

'I'm not homeless,' replied Grandma.

'Whatever,' said Rosie's dad. 'Officer. *Ahem.* Chop-chop. I'm a busy man. No time to lose.'

'She's not technically doing anything wrong,' said the policewoman, as calmly as she could. She didn't look as though she liked Rosie's dad too much either.

'Well, she's *technically* making my shopping centre look bad,' he muttered under his breath. 'Why is everyone trying to ruin my life?'

He took a deep breath and massaged his eyes.

'Right,' he said, giving up on the police officer

and turning to us. 'Time's money, so I'm only going to say this once. You lot will stand outside the shopping centre. Do not steal anything or go near my clean windows with your grubby fingers. Her Royal Highness will roll up in her car and shake a few hands. The three lucky children will step forward and hand her some flowers. Then you'll all get lost so the princess can meet me, which is the main reason why she's coming, of course. The rest of you will stay out of the way. I'll whizz her inside and she'll go and buy her badge for the badgers or whatever. Then she'll get back in the car and go home, hopefully without any of you lot touching her. Got it?'

We all nodded.

'Right. Who's going to meet the princess along with my Rosie?' he said, clapping his hands to get our attention.

Vanya and I put our hands up.

Rosie's dad looked at me in disgust. 'You are kidding me. Him? Wearing *that*?'

'I'm not bother—' I began but Rosie interrupted.

'No, Daddy,' simpered Rosie, 'I think Roman looks wonderful. And I know the princess will find him adoramazing.'

I gulped.

'Whatever you say, sugarplum,' he replied. 'The most important thing is that the cameras can see the signs for the shopping centre. He's nice and stumpy so at least he won't block them out.'

'Thanks a bunch,' I said.

'OK. Let's do a run-through. Rosie, other girl and short, weird kid. Come and stand here. Rest of you, buzz off. And, you,' he called over to a workman and clapped his hands, 'get over here and pretend to be the princess. Yes, now. This week'd be good.'

And so we did a last-minute run-through of the princess's visit. It all seemed to go smoothly. Well, apart from the fact that, instead of a beautiful, elegant princess, we had a muscular, tattooed skinhead with a massive gut whose trousers kept slipping down to reveal the top of his bottom. Rosie elbowed me out of the way and pretended to give the workman some flowers. Then he did a really unladylike curtsey and stomped off towards the shop.

Rosie's dad clapped his hands. 'Great. Now remember. Don't mess this up. This is all about advertising my shopping centre.'

'*Ahem*. And the badgers,' said Vanya.

'Yeah, yeah,' said Rosie's dad, waving her away.

'Princess now entering the town centre,' hissed a voice on a police officer's radio.

The news rippled through the crowd.

In the distance we could hear a murmur of cheering and clapping as the royal car passed the crowds on its way towards us.

'Action stations!' called Rosie's dad, before scuttling off to just inside the front door.

Fidgeting nervously, the class stood in a group to one side, while Rosie, Vanya and I positioned ourselves next to the red carpet, right by the entrance to the shopping centre.

My tummy was flipping. My knees felt weak.

The clapping and cheering got closer and louder.

I nervously looked upwards and took a deep breath.

And that's when I saw him.

Gamble.

Meeting the Princess

I knew it was him straight away, even though he was on the first floor of the multistorey car park over the road – I'd recognise that little bald head anywhere. He was peering over the barrier, along with his brother. As the excitement on the street built to fever pitch, they both ducked down again out of sight.

What are they doing? I wondered.

But before I could come up with an answer, Rosie elbowed me in the ribs. 'Roman. Focus. You're meant to be making me look good.'

My eyes dropped to street level and – *holy swiss rolls* – Princess Lucy's car had appeared.

The Rolls Royce pulled up at the end of the red carpet, the royal family's flags fluttering on the bonnet. The car was flanked by six police motorbikes and a whole bunch of burly security guards on foot, who were wearing black suits, sunglasses and earpieces. The car door opened and a long, elegant leg slid out, followed by the rest of the princess. Thousands of cameras clicked and flashed and there was a loud gasp from the crowd; she was so beautiful it was like everyone had been simultaneously punched in the stomach.

Followed at a cautious distance by the police and security guards, Princess Lucy slowly made her way along the red carpet, flashing her white-toothed, pink-lipsticked smile the whole way. It was really weird seeing someone so famous so close up. It almost made me feel dizzy. She moved closer and closer towards us. A ruffle of a baby's hair, a warm handshake for an old man in a wheelchair with medals across his chest, a nod of agreement and a polite laugh to a middle-aged lady, a curtsey towards our class, who were cheering louder than anyone.

'OMG, Youtube fans – I am officially freaking out!' exclaimed Rosie into her phone.

'Put it away,' hissed Mrs McDonald.

Rosie tutted and shoved her phone into her handbag just as the princess reached us. Vanya had been given the flowers, and she held them out towards Princess Lucy.

'Why, thank you. How sweet,' said the princess, handing the flowers back to the closest security guard. Her voice was beautiful and soft, like warm jam oozing out of the side of a doughnut. 'And *my my*, what a simply gorgeous outfit!'

I was so dumbstruck it took me about three seconds to realise she was talking to me. 'Yes. It's a . . . er . . . badger, your royal wonderfulness.'

Royal wonderfulness? Where did that come

from? My palms were so sweaty you could've surfed on them.

'Quite,' said the princess, smiling in the same way you'd smile at a deformed kitten. She turned to one of the security guards. 'I think this young child deserves the first badger badge.'

'What an honour!' sighed Grandma from the crowd.

Oh wow! I thought, biting my lip and glancing excitedly at Vanya, who giggled back.

The princess turned away for a moment. She took a badge from the security guard, unpinned it and attached it to the front of my badger onesie, right on the patch of the old crumper.

I looked over to the crowd. Grandma was practically exploding with excitement and pride. *I* was the first person ever to get a special badger badge from the most famous woman on the planet. What an honour! In ordinary circumstances, I might've felt extremely proud. I might even have fainted with delight.

But these were not ordinary circumstances.

Because, at the exact moment when she clipped the little badger badge onto me, two things happened.

1) I saw something. Something utterly terrible. 'Sweet sugary sprinkles,' I whispered. The princess's beautiful forehead crinkled up into a frown. 'Excuse me?' she asked. But before I could explain . . .

↓

2) Rosie Taylor shoulder-barged me out of the way so hard that I fell to the floor.

'Your Royal Highness, I'm not sure you wish to fraternise with commoners like him,' Rosie twittered.

'Oh my . . .' said the princess, looking from Rosie to me and back again. I noticed that she was holding the badge in her hand. It was still attached to the patch of crumper, which had been ripped off my chest when Rosie whacked into me. A single thread of wool joined it to my onesie.

Rosie carried on talking breathlessly. 'Yes you see, Your Highness, or can I call you Lucy, or even Luce because we can be friends from now on and . . .'

I was barely listening. And that was because the very terrible thing I mentioned was getting closer.

I'd seen it emerge ten seconds earlier from the multistorey car park. At first I'd hoped it was a mirage or maybe that I was seeing things.

But it was very real, and shooting straight towards us at incredible speed.

And because everyone else's eyes were on the princess, I was the only person who'd seen it until it was right above us.

Vanya was next to notice. 'Is that . . . ?'

She didn't have time to finish because the terrible thing was now hovering inches above Princess Lucy's head. As its shadow spread across the pavement, the princess looked up. Then she screamed.

Directly above her was Spud Gamble's drone. And dangling face to face with her from underneath it was a fully grown badger.

A flipping *badger*, for crying out loud! It was just swinging there like a massive, smelly yo-yo.

Tied to its tail, a long piece of material trailed behind it with 'SAVE HOPPALONG' written on it in big red letters.

Within seconds the crowd noticed it and there

was total chaos. People were screaming. Cameras were flashing again.

Princess Lucy's security guards were talking urgently into their headsets and panicking. What could they do? I'm sure they were highly trained, but it's not like they could ever have made plans for how to deal with a massive flying badger, is it? And anyway, this was a *badger charity* event – I don't think it would've gone down too well if they'd shot it out of the sky.

Rosie's dad was absolutely furious. He tried to knock the badger to the ground with a broom but Princess Lucy turned to him in disgust. 'Stop that at once, you ghastly man!'

And then, another awful thing happened.

While everyone was looking at the drone and the dangling badger and Rosie's dad (who was now bowing down on the ground and grovelling in front of the princess), there was a loud 'AAAACCCCHH-HHHOOOOOOOO!'

Then the whole world seemed to stop.

Good grief.

Rosie Taylor had sneezed all over Princess Lucy.

It was a proper humdinger as well – a massive

shower of snot and spit that speckled Princess Lucy's dress from top to bottom.

Now, I'm not an expert on how you're meant to act in front of royalty but I'm pretty certain that sneezing on them is not the right thing to do. The crowd froze. Rosie's eyes nearly burst out of her head. 'I'm so sorry!' she begged, 'it's the badger and . . .'

Wow – it turned out she really *was* allergic to animals after all!

Princess Lucy took a step backwards, staring at Rosie in a mixture of horror and revulsion. In fact, she was so disturbed by what was going on that she was still holding onto the patch of crumper. I felt the strand of wool tightening. A couple of stitches popped out.

'Er . . . Your Majesty,' I began, trying to tug the strand of wool back from her.

But she didn't notice me because, as if things weren't bad enough, a voice rang out across the road. 'Alright, Princess!'

In the confusion, nobody had noticed Gamble hopping over the fence and running towards us. When he reached the princess, he swiped his finger across his phone screen to lower the drone to the ground. Unfortunately for me, this caused Hoppalong the badger to crash into my chest, pinning me to the ground.

'It's going to eat me!' I cried, but my voice was muffled by a massive mouthful of badger. And anyway, it didn't *actually* eat me. What happened next was much, much worse.

Hoppalong seemed to fall in love with me.

I mean, I know that badgers are shortsighted, and I *was* dressed like one, but come on! It was completely gross. Hoppalong started nuzzling my neck, snuffling at me with its stinky breath. Then it crawled across my chest, turned around, shoved its bum in my face and squirted out some utterly disgusting liquid at me.

'That's called musk,' said Gamble, unhelpfully, as I spluttered and coughed. 'They do that when they fancy you.'

I lay there holding my breath and wiping my streaming eyes as Vanya pulled the badger off me by the harness. It strained against it like a dog, still panting and grunting excitedly at me. I don't speak badger, but I'm pretty certain it was saying: 'Hey, hot stuff. Fancy a snog?'

Meanwhile Rosie was still begging Princess Lucy

for forgiveness and dabbing her dress with a hanky. And as if this wasn't bad enough for her, Gamble had detached the digital camera from the drone and was waving it in front of the princess's face. Still holding onto the badge and my patch of crumper, the princess edged away even further, pulling more and more stitches out of the front of my onesie.

'Before we talk about saving Hoppalong, can I have a selfie with you?' Gamble asked, putting his arm round her.

Four security guards immediately leapt on Gamble and bundled him to the floor, sending the digital camera skittering along the ground. I think the princess was about to scream, but she was interrupted by a tinny voice from the speaker on the camera.

'I've been through hell this week just so I can meet the princess . . . I've had to raise money for stinking, disgusting animals,' said the voice. I recognised it instantly. *Rosie.* But where had I heard those words before? Then it dawned on me: at the park yesterday. The camera must've been recording when Rosie was ranting at me. Of course! What had Spud said the other day? *It's got an HD video camera that could film a flea up-close from two miles away. The play button must've been pressed when it landed on the ground.*

'Who on earth would say such horrific things?' said Princess Lucy.

Rosie's face was now a mask of complete terror. 'No. No. I'm sorry, Your Majesterialness. I can explain.'

Princess Lucy stormed past her and snatched up the camera from the ground. She was still holding the badge, and this caused another row of stitches to pop out of my onesie.

As Princess Lucy stared at the tiny screen in disbelief, Rosie's voice continued out of the speaker: '. . . I *hate* animals. I don't want to keep them safe. They're almost as vile as you! If I could, I'd line up every badger in Britain and run them over in Daddy's Range Rover. In fact . . .'

Princess Lucy turned to Rosie. 'You nasty, horrible little turd!' she snapped.

The crowd all went *ooooooh.*

Rosie looked like a balloon that'd just been popped.

Even though I loved hearing the princess say this, I have to say it wasn't very princessy. Plus it was hard to enjoy it too much as Hoppalong had squirmed out of Vanya's grasp and was now cuddling my ankle and licking my leg.

And at that moment, the security guards decided that enough was enough. They bundled the princess away towards her Rolls Royce. Within seconds, she was safely inside. The car doors were slammed shut. The engine revved. The tyres screeched and she shot away.

'NOOOOOOO!' screamed Rosie, sinking to her knees.

But if things were bad for her, they were a million times worse for me.

Because it was at that precise moment that I realised Princess Lucy was still holding onto the patch of crumper. And the stitches of the onesie were unravelling rapidly. It was disappearing before my eyes, row by row. First the chest and the back. Then the arms and the legs. And before I knew it, I was standing there – in the middle of the street, in front of thousands of people and the world's media – wearing just a badger mask and my pants.

'Oh nuggets,' I sighed, as a thousand cameras flashed and clicked.

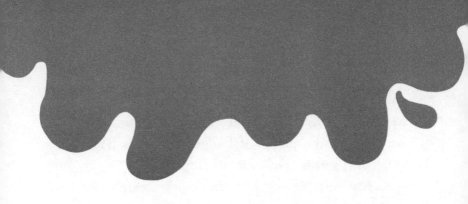

Epilogue

I was so embarrassed afterwards that I didn't watch TV or look on the internet for a whole week, but Gamble gleefully told me that the video 'Naked Badger Boy' had been all over the news and now had twice as many online views as 'Cow Toilet Girl'.

I was a worldwide sensation.

At first I thought that this would be a bad thing, but actually, after a few days, it all turned out really well. Luckily, you couldn't see my face in the video, so not too many people recognised me when I was out and about. Also, Badges for Badgers got so much publicity from the video that it raised ten million pounds in the first four days. I even got sent a golden badger badge by the Princess's private secretary for my 'personal sacrifices in drawing attention to the plight of badgers'. This is posh-speak for 'getting your kit off in public'.

As for Rosie, she and her mum flew straight out to Barbados afterwards and she hasn't been seen since. I only know this because, according to Vanya, Rosie's fashion blog has closed down and been replaced by the message:

> Sorry, fans. I know that this blog is the best thing in some of your lives, but I am taking a break from fame until all of this blows over.

Hopefully that will take several decades.

However the best thing about all this was that Rosie's dad came round to my house a couple of days later. He was absolutely delighted. Apparently, business at the shopping centre was booming because of me. People were coming from all over Europe to have their photos taken outside and to spend loads of cash. He handed me an envelope and said, 'Don't tell Rosie about this when she gets back, but thank you. I always reward people who make me loads of money.' Once he'd climbed back into his Range Rover and driven off, I looked inside the envelope. There was a hundred-pound voucher for the shopping centre in there. Seriously. A hundred quid!

Immediately I thought: *I could buy a whole pile of clothes with it then I'll never have to wear any of Grandma's knitted rubbish again.* But then again . . . like I said at the start, there are way more important things than clothes. And, of course, Rosie's dad's shopping centre *does* have that massive Squidgy Splodge Doughnut shop. A hundred quid would keep me in doughnuts for . . . *oooh* . . . at least a day. And I could probably afford a little present for Grandma as well.

Meanwhile, Rosie's dad and I weren't the only ones who did well out of the publicity. A badger-lover from a few miles away saw the news and adopted Hoppalong. He now lives in a special badger sanctuary in this person's garden, where he pulls himself along on a skateboard. Gamble Skypes him every morning before school. Apparently, Hoppalong has also now met a new badger girlfriend, which is a bit of a relief frankly.

So, everything turned out brilliantly.

Well. Almost.

The only bird poo on the ice cream was Grandma. She was so thrilled that Princess Lucy had called the badger costume 'adorable' that she'd gone straight home and hadn't stopped knitting since. She phoned our house last night. 'I've made you lots of lovely new outfits, Roman,' she told me. 'In fact, there are so many your dad might need to hire a lorry to come and collect them.'

I gulped. 'How . . . *lovely*.'

MARK LOWERY grew up in Preston but now lives near Cambridge with his young family. Some of the time he is a primary school teacher. In the olden days he used to spend his time doing lots of active stuff like running, hiking, snowboarding and swimming but now he prefers staying in and attempting to entertain his children. He plays the guitar badly and speaks appalling Italian but he knows a lot about biscuits. In his mind he is one of the great footballers of his generation, although he is yet to demonstrate this on an actual football pitch. He has an MA in Writing for Children and his first two books were both shortlisted for the Roald Dahl Funny Prize. He is yet to find a cake that he doesn't like.

Find out more at
www.marklowery.co.uk

Piccadilly
P R E S S

Thank you for choosing a Piccadilly Press book.

If you would like to know more about our authors, our books or if you'd just like to know what we're up to, you can find us online.

www.piccadillypress.co.uk

You can also find us on:

We hope to see you soon!